THE STUDENT

JOHN NICHOLL

B
Boldwood

First published in 2019. This edition first published in Great Britain in 2022 by Boldwood Books Ltd.

Copyright © John Nicholl, 2019

Cover Design by Head Design Ltd

Cover Photography: Shutterstock

The moral right of John Nicholl to be identified as the author of this work has been asserted in accordance with the Copyright, Designs and Patents Act 1988.

All rights reserved. No part of this book may be reproduced in any form or by any electronic or mechanical means, including information storage and retrieval systems, without written permission from the author, except for the use of brief quotations in a book review.

This book is a work of fiction and, except in the case of historical fact, any resemblance to actual persons, living or dead, is purely coincidental.

Every effort has been made to obtain the necessary permissions with reference to copyright material, both illustrative and quoted. We apologise for any omissions in this respect and will be pleased to make the appropriate acknowledgements in any future edition.

A CIP catalogue record for this book is available from the British Library.

Paperback ISBN 978-1-80426-389-1

Large Print ISBN 978-1-80426-388-4

Hardback ISBN 978-1-80426-390-7

Ebook ISBN 978-1-80426-387-7

Kindle ISBN 978-1-80426-386-0

Audio CD ISBN 978-1-80426-395-2

MP3 CD ISBN 978-1-80426-394-5

Digital audio download ISBN 978-1-80426-392-1

Boldwood Books Ltd
23 Bowerdean Street
London SW6 3TN
www.boldwoodbooks.com

1

Harry Gilmore sat on the town hall steps and frowned as the throng of weekend shoppers went about their business, seemingly oblivious to his existence.

He dabbed at one eye, and then the other, with the sleeve of his university sweatshirt, before reading the offending text for the third time in a matter of minutes. 'It's over.' That's how it began. After nine happy months, she'd dumped him. And she hadn't even had the decency to do it face-to-face, when he could beg or plead or throw himself on her mercy. He loved her. He'd always love her. His feelings were sincere and genuine. That's what he told himself. He'd known she was the one the very first time he saw her standing at the students' union bar, with her tight jeans and red cotton T-shirt clinging to her curves. Simone was the girl of his dreams. What the hell was he going to do without the one person that made his life worth living?

Harry seriously considered drafting a carefully considered response explaining exactly how he felt. Something emotive, something heartfelt, a reply she couldn't ignore. A message that left her in no doubt that he wanted her back. But what would that achieve?

Why give the girl the satisfaction of knowing she'd torn his heart to pieces? She didn't love him. She'd never loved him, not really, not in the adult, grown-up way that he loved her. She'd made that perfectly clear in unambiguous language he couldn't fail to understand, as if his feelings meant nothing to her. As if she was grinding his emotions into the gutter for the sheer pleasure of it all. And she'd met someone new. The dagger in his back. The final nail in their relationship's coffin, before it was lowered into the ground forever. She'd met her soulmate. Her soulmate! She'd actually used the word. And they were going travelling together for the summer, Thailand, Cambodia and maybe Vietnam too. Something she'd always wanted to do, apparently. Really? Wasn't it strange how she'd never mentioned anything of the kind? Not a hint, not even once in the months they'd been together. Maybe they were *his* words. The new man in her life.

Harry shook his head as his melancholy thoughts pounded him down a little further. She never did have much imagination. Maybe the bastard had written it for her. She never was very original. *Yeah, it's probably him.*

Harry stuffed his smartphone into a back pocket of his blue jeans, rolled a cigarette, a recently acquired habit he still thought cool despite a tightening chest. He lit the tip and coughed as he sucked the toxic fumes deep into his lungs, blowing it from his mouth and watching it swirl. He checked his pockets for change, swore crudely under his breath, and began making his way towards the nearest student pub, a few minutes' walk away. He wasn't a great drinker, as he was never sure how alcohol would interact with the antidepressants he relied on to stabilise his moods. But he felt that after this setback a few drinks would take the edge off things, and he hadn't experienced a real low for some months now. He could afford a couple of pints at best if there was a discount on offer. Perhaps he'd bump into a mate, who'd lend him a tenner to drown his sorrows. But probably not, given his luck. *Could life get any better? Yes, it fucking well could. What a cow! What a total and utter bitch! Sending a text! A fucking text after nine happy months! I am well rid of her. I can do better, can't I? Yeah, of course I can. Her loss!*

He trudged on and sighed. Who the hell was he trying to kid? He'd never felt more miserable in his entire life. The girl meant everything to him. He'd do anything to get her back.

2

The two young women and their older male companion sat in an old, rust-pocked Transit van dressed entirely in white, scanning the street with keen eyes, as they had for almost two hours.

Achara, a dark-haired, strikingly attractive young woman, peered to her right. 'What about him?'

The big man swivelled in the driver's seat, tugging at an unkempt brown beard tinged with grey as he pressed his face against the glass. 'Which one?'

Achara pointed with a purple-painted fingernail that perfectly complimented her slender hand. 'Him, him, the guy in the faded jeans and black top. He's been crying. Look at the state of his eyes. That's got to be a good sign, easy-peasy. He's young, he looks reasonably fit. He'd make an ideal manual worker. We couldn't find a better target.'

The big man lifted his military binoculars to his eyes and focussed on Harry's face. 'It could be hay fever. It's the time of year for it. You're making assumptions based on dubious evidence. Maybe he hasn't been crying at all.'

Achara made a face, frustrated by the big man's lack of trust in her ability. 'Look at his hunched shoulders, the morose expression on his face. He's perfect, absolutely perfect. Just give me a chance. That's all I'm asking. Let me prove myself. Surely I've earned that much after all this time.'

The man lowered the binoculars, sighing as he rested them on his lap. 'I don't know. I'm not so sure.'

Achara kept her eyes on Harry as she responded, her initial frustration fast becoming agitation that threatened to boil to the surface. 'I'm here to serve the master, but how can I do that if you never give me the chance to prove myself worthy. It's been months since I completed the training. I'm ready and waiting. If not now, when?'

The big man took a deep intake of breath and exhaled slowly, weighing up his options as the second young woman spoke for the first time in over an hour. 'Oh, come on, Baptist, Achara knows what she's doing. She's completed the course. She passed with flying colours, a natural. One of the best we've ever had. You said that yourself. Achara's got it spot on. You've got to learn to trust her. The boy will be gone if we don't get a move on. It's time to let her fly.'

Baptist lifted the binoculars to his eyes for a second time, focussing on Harry, confirming his downbeat persona and nodding reticently. 'Okay, go on, out you go. He's approaching the top of the hill. Near the charity shop on the left. You'll catch up with him easily enough if you hurry. I'll be back here and waiting at 2.30 p.m. sharp. Do not be late. There's no room for errors. This is far too important for that.'

Achara broke into a smile that lit up her face as she pushed the passenger side door open and stepped out into the sunshine, as excited as a child on a birthday morning. 'Thank you, thank you so very much. I won't let you down.'

'Have you got the drug?'

She glanced back at him, patting a trouser pocket and grimacing, disappointed that he felt the need to ask. 'Of course. It's here safe and sound.'

'You're certain?'

Her frustration was betrayed by her tone. 'Yes, a thousand times, yes.'

'Pass this one final test, and you can move up a level in the community. It doesn't get any better than that. Make the most of the opportunity. The master doesn't tolerate failure. Remember that; carve it in tablets of stone. Screw this up, and it won't go well for either of us.'

3

Harry sat alone in the quiet bar, head bowed, sipping his ice-cold lager, making it last, rather than gulping it down as he would have wished. Drowning your sorrows wasn't an option when you were skint, with a few miserable coins in your pocket and no notes.

Harry's mind was filled with melancholy thoughts, coming in waves, one after another, dragging him down a little further, when he was suddenly distracted, his busy mind silenced in the blink of an eye. He looked up and stared as one of the most beautiful young women he'd ever seen walked towards him in what seemed like a dream, a fantasy brought to life. He opened his eyes wide and studied her, forgetting his sadness in an instant, drinking in her image: her lithe body, her long, black silky hair, her piercing almond eyes, and best of all, loose white cotton trousers that left almost everything to his overactive imagination.

Maybe Simone had been right about him looking at other girls when they were together. Perhaps she'd had a point despite his protestations to the contrary. Maybe she was correct to leave him for somebody else. She'd said he was driven by his hormones. Maybe it was true.

Harry drove his ex from his mind, as the girl slowly approached him with a seductive smile playing on her very pretty face. He looked her up and down again and lingered, trying not to be too obvious and failing miserably, as she continued to stroll towards him one slow step at a time. Harry fully expected the vision of beauty to walk straight past him, as if she hadn't noticed him at all, but instead, she stopped immediately in front of him, meeting his gaze as he searched for something appropriate to say. Some form of apology for staring perhaps, or maybe nothing at all.

'Is it okay if I sit down?'

Harry swallowed a mouthful of lager, glancing to left and right to confirm she really was talking to him, before breaking into a lopsided grin and nodding once. There had to be a catch. Surely there had to be a catch. He licked his top lip and spoke, fearing the words would stick in his throat, attempting to sound as relaxed as possible but feeling entirely out of his depth. 'Yeah, yeah, it's a free country, but if you're selling something, you're wasting your time. I'm a poor student, totally skint. It goes with the territory.'

She rolled her eyes and laughed. 'And there was me thinking you're a successful businessman with a villa in the Med and oodles of money in the bank. You know, like Rockefeller, Trump, or someone like that. It must have been the sweatshirt, tattered jeans and worn-out trainers that did it. Don't tell me my rich radar's playing up again. I'll have to get it repaired and meet a millionaire.'

Harry sipped his drink and grinned self-consciously, still thinking she must have some unstated agenda but desperately hoping she hadn't. He placed a hand in a front pocket of his jeans and took out a handful of loose change, mostly coppers. 'I think I've probably got just about enough to buy you a drink if you fancy one. As long as you choose something cheap, nothing expensive.'

She shook her head and gestured to the middle-aged barman, who ignored an overweight drunk's demands for attention and responded with a degree of enthusiasm he hadn't experienced in quite some time. 'What can I get you, love?'

'I'll have a glass of white wine and another pint of whatever my new friend's drinking. He looks as if he could do with it.'

'Sweet or dry, the wine, sweet or dry?'

'Dry, please, I'm sweet enough.'

The barman ran his tongue across his top lip. 'You certainly are.' She handed him a crisp ten-pound note, waited for her change, and approached a table for two located almost directly below a wall-mounted jukebox. 'Will you bring them over?'

It wasn't usually part of the service, but how could he refuse? 'Yeah, no probs, take a seat, love.' He began pouring cheap supermarket wine into a reasonably clean glass with an unsteady hand. 'Give me a second, love. I'll be with you before you know it.'

Harry picked up his glass, tilted his head back and drained it, Dutch courage to boost his flagging confidence just when he felt he needed it most. He slotted a single fifty pence coin into the jukebox, selecting two tracks he thought suitable, before joining her at the table. What was it that she really wanted? Surely there had to be something. Yeah, of course there was. He'd never been that lucky, not even once in his life.

Harry was still questioning her motives as he took his seat, despite her friendly demeanour. Her smile, that lovely smile, unnerved him in some way he couldn't fully process. He wanted to study her face, to drink in her image, to drown in those eyes, but he felt obliged to look away. She appeared unattainable, way out of his league, on a different level to him entirely. Not like any girl he'd met before. 'If you want me to sign up for some charity, you've picked the wrong man. I'm up to my eyeballs in debt. The government made sure of that. I can just about manage to feed myself. I've got nothing to spare.'

She swayed rhythmically, first to one side and then the other, graceful, elegant, refined, as a sweeping electric guitar solo filled the air with sound. 'I don't care how much money you've got. I'm just looking for some company. I needed someone to talk to in a lonely world. Why are you finding that so hard to accept? Don't you believe in befriending strangers? The world would seem a better place if you did.'

Harry looked up and nodded in acknowledgement as the drooling barman delivered the drinks to the table with a gap-toothed grin, nicotine-yellowed teeth in full view as he hovered over them, trying to glance down her top. 'Do you want anything else? There's pies or pasties if you fancy one? I could heat them up in the microwave.'

Harry glanced at his new companion, who shook her head, screwing up her face. 'No, that's everything, thanks.'

Harry returned his attention to the girl, who was sipping her wine just a few drops at a time. He was gaining confidence now, more full of himself, but there were still doubts. Nagging doubts he couldn't shake off. 'Okay, so you wanted someone to talk to, I get that. But, why me of all people?'

She giggled nervously, thinking her mission was proving significantly more challenging than she'd expected, despite the months of training. It had all seemed so very easy in role play, so natural, a piece of cake. But real life was proving a very different proposition. She had to relax, focus. Put what she'd learnt to good use. Failure was too terrible to even contemplate. 'I'm new to the area. You've got a friendly face. Why not you? Everyone's a stranger until you get to know them. My lovely mum taught me that.'

Harry laughed self-consciously. 'Why not me? How many reasons do you want? I can think of a few.'

She raised an eyebrow. 'Okay, you've got me. I saw you crying on the steps. You looked as if you could do with cheering up. Think of it as my good deed for the day. I'm high on life. Why not share the joy? And if I make a new friend in the process, well, hooray to that. It's a win-win.'

Harry looked away, acutely aware of his red, bloodshot eyes, knowing he wasn't looking his best. He briefly considered rushing to the men's room to splash cold water on his face. But he relaxed slightly, looking at her with a newfound sense of hope when she reached across the table and touched his hand. 'So basically, you felt sorry for me. It's a sympathy chat. Is that what you're saying?'

She laughed, head back, smiling, keen to lighten the mood. 'Yes, if that's how you want to put it.'

'I'm not suicidal if that's what you're thinking. I'm having a bad day, but I'm not a charity case.'

She tensed, muscles taut, drumming a thigh with the fingers of one hand. She was losing him. It was time to change tack. Play the needy female. Show some vulnerability. This had to be convincing. 'No, no, I didn't think that for a moment. You've got a friendly face, that's all, like I said. I was feeling a little lonely, and I decided to say hello. I'm not in the habit of approaching strange men in bars. It's not something I've ever done before. It was an instinctive thing, a one-off. I just felt we had a connection. I know that probably sounds ridiculous in your very different world. But it's as if I'd met you somewhere before.'

Harry nodded, satisfied with her explanation, counting his blessings. Ready and willing to accept almost anything she said and at any cost. 'I don't even know your name.'

'Achara, it's Thai. It means Angel. My mum came to the UK to marry my father about a year before I was born.'

'Anchara?'

She repeated it, clearly enunciating each letter, emphasising the absence of an N.

He smiled with his eyes. 'It's a lovely name, beautiful. It suits you perfectly.'

'Thank you! I like it too. What about yours?'

'Nothing so exotic, I'm afraid. It's Harry, Harry Gilmore, I'm a student at the university.'

She pointed at the large white logo emblazoned on the front of his black top, nodding once before pushing her hair away from her face with a mischievous grin. 'Yeah, I'd worked that out for myself. I'm not a complete numpty. What are you studying?'

He paused before responding. She was so attractive, so very beautiful, almost perfect. 'I've just completed the first year of a sociology degree.'

'How's it going? Are you enjoying the course?'

'Um, yeah, it's okay, I guess, it's interesting enough. I didn't work nearly as hard as I should have for the end of year exams. But I still think I'll do okay. Fingers crossed! I'll find out my results in a few weeks' time... what about you? What brings you to this part of the world?'

'I'm British, I was born here. Mum's Thai but Dad's Welsh, he's from Cardiff.'

Harry gritted his teeth, rubbing the back of his neck, admonishing himself for his stupidity. 'No, no, I didn't mean anything like that. You said you were new to the area. I just wondered what brought you to Carmarthen, that's all. Your accent doesn't sound local. I didn't mean to imply...'

She looked at him, weighing him up, trying to read his thoughts as he squirmed in his chair. 'I'd stop digging if I were you. I know exactly what you meant. You don't need to explain yourself.'

Harry's face reddened. 'Yeah, sorry, I don't know what the hell's wrong with me sometimes.'

'If you give me a chance, I'll teach you how to relax.'

'That would be nice.'

'So why the tears when I first saw you? What was that about?'

Harry averted his eyes to the wall as his second song began

playing on the jukebox. *Why choose a ballad? A love song! What the hell was I thinking?* 'I'd had some bad news.'

She frowned, made her eyes sad, pressed her lips together. 'Oh, I'm sorry to hear that. What sort of bad news? I hope you don't mind me asking.'

Harry lowered his head. 'Oh, I, err, I don't really want to talk about it.'

Achara lifted her glass to her mouth and sipped. Buying time to think. She noted his vulnerability, his apparent emotional fragility, and decided now was precisely the right time to drive home her advantage. To flutter her eyelids, to flatter him, to reel him in. 'Was it something to do with a girl?'

Harry blushed crimson. 'What makes you think that?'

She studied his face and knew she was winning. 'You're young, you're quite good looking, it just seems the most obvious explanation. I bet you get a lot of female attention. I'm right, aren't I?'

It was far from true, but he decided to go with it. 'Um, yeah, yeah, I guess so, but not usually from anyone as nice as you.'

She laughed. He was so predictable, so transparent. 'So, was it a girl who made you cry?'

Harry briefly considered lying, but he decided against it at the last second. Instead, he chose his words with care, hoping he wouldn't blow it, determining a measure of honesty was his best policy. It seemed good to start as he meant to go on. 'Oh, she's just a girl I thought I loved. She's met someone new. They're going travelling together. He's the future, and I'm the past. Now that I think about it, I don't think she was the right person for me at all... how about you? Are you in a relationship?'

She looked deep into his eyes, shaking her head to left and right, ever so slowly, ever so gracefully. 'No, there's no one. I've been waiting to meet the right man.'

Harry moved to the very edge of his seat, resting his elbows on the table, telling himself something could come of their meeting. That he may have won the relationship lottery. 'Do you mean someone like me?'

She smiled without parting her lips. She had him, hook, line and sinker. 'I believe in fate, in the mysteries of the universe. I believe we were destined to meet.'

He pulled his head back. 'Really?'

Achara nodded assuredly. 'Oh, yes, all that's gone before was leading us to this precise moment in time. God's looking down on us both and smiling right now. I've never been more certain of anything in my life. Everything's just as it should be. As it was meant to be. Can you feel it, Harry? Because I can. It's in the air. Love is all around.'

Harry's breathing deepened, his heart rate increasing as he pictured her naked. What the hell could he say to that? 'Shall I put some more music on the jukebox? I think I've got one last fifty pence coin here somewhere.'

She pushed her glass aside, tilting her head at a slight angle. 'Are you changing the subject, my new friend?'

Harry opened his mouth as if to speak, but then closed it again, momentarily lost for words as she rose to her feet, every movement of her body a work of art.

'Were you going to say something?'

'I was just thinking you're not like anyone I've ever met before.'

Achara smiled. 'Different in a good way?'

'Oh, yes, definitely in a good way!'

'Come on, up you get. I'm feeling peckish all of a sudden.'

Harry's face fell. 'I'm completely skint.'

'That's not a problem, it's my treat.'

'Are you sure?'

She reached down, taking his hand in hers, lifting him to his feet. 'I offered, didn't I?'

'Yeah, I guess you did.'

'Is there a veggie place here in town?'

'Um, there is an Italian place my mum and dad used to take me to on special occasions back in the day. I don't know how much vegetarian stuff they do, but it's nice enough from what I remember.'

'I'm a strict vegan. I don't eat anything of animal origin. Can you think of anywhere else? That's not going to be a problem, is it?'

Harry was an enthusiastic meat eater, his tastes more bacon roll than quinoa, but he was never going to admit it, not now, not to her. 'No, no, not at all, I *love* vegetarian food, always have. I can't get enough of the stuff.'

She squeezed his hand. 'So, do you know of anywhere?'

Harry counted to three inside his head, trying to think about anything other than sex as they walked out into the sunshine. 'There is a small vegetarian café in Merlin's Lane. I haven't been there myself, but I've heard good things. One of my mates mentioned it. He goes to an open mic night at the end of each month. I keep meaning to try it myself.'

Achara looked at him and smiled warmly. 'Well, now's your chance. Come on, you can lead the way.'

4

Achara looked around the atmospheric, lilac-painted café, its four walls hung with colourful paintings by talented local artists. The place had a bohemian feel she liked immediately. It would have been a pleasant place to spend an hour or two, eating, drinking and chatting with like-minded friends. But she had a job to do. She had to concentrate. She had to stay focussed. She was there for a purpose. She couldn't let herself forget that even for a single second.

Not now that she seemed so very close to success.

Achara pointed towards a black, faux leather settee in one corner of the room close to the serving counter and smiled. 'That looks comfortable. What do you think? How about there?'

Harry nodded and sat himself down, making room for his new companion, still not quite able to believe his luck. She seemed so way out of his league, a ten as opposed to his five, on a different level entirely. He picked up a green cardboard menu and handed it to her before perusing a second one himself.

Achara placed her menu back on the low table 'Anything you fancy?'

'I think I'll just have the soup.'

She turned her head to face him. 'I want you to choose whatever you like. It's not expensive. My treat, remember? Don't feel you have to go for the cheapest option on the menu. I wouldn't want that. We're here to enjoy ourselves.'

Harry screwed up his face. 'Are you sure?'

'Yes, how many times do I have to say it? You can pay next time if that makes you feel better.'

He smiled from ear to ear, making no effort to hide his pleasure. 'There's going to be a next time?'

'Yes, why not? We get on well enough. We seem to have a natural affinity. I'd like to come again, wouldn't you?'

Harry nodded eagerly. 'Yeah, absolutely, let's make it happen.'

She touched his arm and lingered as a pretty young waitress with bright red hair and hoop earrings approached the table.

'Are you ready to order, guys?'

Harry waited for Achara to choose first, and then said he'd have the same, feigning enthusiasm, focussing more on her than his desire for sustenance.

Achara grinned, reading him like a large print book. Things were going better than she could ever have hoped. The grooming process was proving easier by the minute. Just like the scenarios she'd acted out time and again in training. Men really were such predictable creatures. Precisely as she'd been told. Why did she ever doubt it? The boy seemed as malleable as warm clay. 'So, are you going to tell me more about the girl who made you cry?'

Harry raised a hand to his face, shielding his eyes. 'Um, I'd err, I'd rather forget about her, if that's all right with you?'

She sat looking at him in quiet contemplation for a few seconds before speaking again. 'That was exactly the right thing to say. You're gaining wisdom, Harry. We all have to accept change. It's a part of life's rich journey. You're on a different path now. Let her go with a light heart. It will be easier that way. Why fight it? It wasn't meant to be.'

Harry massaged his gut with one hand, swallowing his sadness, putting on a brave face and thinking of a new future. 'Yeah, sorry, I know all those tears were stupid. We were only going out together for a few months. But she was my first real girlfriend. Rejection can be hard to take. It knocked my ability to trust. I really thought we had a future.'

Achara reached out, gripping his arm, simulating concern with accomplished ease. 'Let her go, Harry. Let her memory fade. Her loss is my gain. There's an affinity between us. Can you feel it? I don't think it's just me. There are better times ahead for both of us. This is day one of many. There are great things to come. Just you wait and see.'

He raised himself upright in his seat, more animated now, keen to lighten the mood. 'Pinch me! This all seems like a dream. You've been so very kind, so understanding. It's been a fantastic couple of hours. I can't quite believe it's happening.'

Achara leant towards him, kissing him gently on his stubbled cheek. 'Oh, it's real all right. Or, at least as real as anything is in this world. All of life is an illusion, a journey of the soul. Just accept it and enjoy the ride.'

Harry had absolutely no idea what she was talking about, but he was never going to admit that, not to her, not now. He smiled his best smile, nodding enthusiastically as if he understood every single word. 'Yeah, yeah, I get what you're saying. I was thinking much the same thing myself. It makes absolute sense. I know exactly what you mean. Nothing happens by accident.'

Achara kissed his face again, more tenderly this time, mouth slightly open with a hint of passion, leaving a small damp patch of warm saliva on his skin.

She relaxed back in her seat, looking at him and only him,

holding him in the palm of her hand. 'Okay, that's agreed. Let's both forget about the past and focus on the future. Let's live in the now. We'll let change happen on both a physical and psychological level. Let my touch awaken your mind and body. Learn to do that, and you'll have the best time of your life. That, I can promise you.'

Harry was shaken by the intensity of his feelings. His entire body felt more alive than ever before. It seemed love at first sight was real. He knew it because it was happening to him. 'Yeah, let's do exactly that. I'm beginning to think today's the most important day of my life.'

'Oh, it is, Harry, it is.'

He noticed that his hands were slightly clammy as the same attentive if unconventional waitress delivered two steaming bowls of aromatic vegetable curry to the table, followed by two tall glasses filled almost to the brim with almond milk banana shakes with cinnamon powder sprinkled on the top.

'Is there anything else I can get you, guys?'

Achara shook her head, smiling warmly, speaking for both of them. 'We're good thanks. It all looks delicious. I'm glad we came.'

'If there's anything else you need, just give me a shout. I won't be far away.'

Harry picked up his fork, moving his food around his bowl, allowing the rising vapour to warm his face as the waitress walked off with a sway of her hips. 'Things like this just don't happen to me. It still feels like a fantasy come true. What seemed like one of the worst days of my life is fast becoming one of the best.'

Achara's eyes widened. 'Only *one* of the best? I thought I was doing better than that.'

He grinned. 'Okay, the best, definitely the best.'

'All of life's a dream, a creation of our mass consciousness. Don't wake up, that's the key. We create our own reality based on our thoughts and emotions. That's how things work, karma, we get exactly what we deserve in this life. Just keep dreaming, think nice thoughts. There's just energy and awareness, that's it. Everything else is a delusion. A profoundly wise man taught me that. Don't be one of life's robots, get off the hamster wheel, open your mind and embrace life's rich tapestry.'

Harry nodded once, still desperate to give the impression they were on the same wavelength. But they really couldn't have been more different. He'd already realised that. He knew it full well. Had she not looked so gorgeous, so alluring, he suspected he'd have walked away long before now. That was the truth of it. But there was something about her. A beauty that drew him to her like a moth to the flame. The last thing he wanted was to spoil the mood. He searched his mind for something to say. Something meaningful, something profound, something to impress. 'How are you liking the curry?' He silently cursed his limitations. *Oh, for fuck's sake! Is that really the best you can do?*

She laughed, contemplating his need for enlightenment. Thinking he had so much to learn. He was such a naive boy, such an innocent. The master would mould him in his image. 'It's lovely, thanks. What about you?'

Harry lifted his glass to his mouth and took a generous gulp of the sweet liquid, oblivious to the thick milky residue it left above his top lip. 'Yeah, it's great, thanks. I really appreciate your generosity.'

She reached out, wiped his mouth with a delicate swipe of her finger, and then licked it clean. 'You don't need to keep thanking me. I'm enjoying your company, that's payment enough. We've agreed you can pay next time. Let's leave it at that.'

He crossed his legs as his penis began to swell. 'The day started off feeling like a total disaster, and now I'm sitting here talking to you with a big grin on my face. It all seems too good to be true. Are you sure there's not something you're not telling me?'

Achara adopted a more serious persona, looking at him with unblinking eyes that seemed to reach out and touch his very soul. 'You need to stop being so cynical. Good things happen to good people. Just accept it. The stars are aligned in your favour. Everything's just as it should be. Exactly like I said before. Just like I told you.'

Harry shook his head, far from persuaded but still wanting to believe every word she said. There was music in her voice. Poetry in every sentence she uttered. He told himself he knew exactly what she wanted to hear. And he was going to say it without fear of contradiction. 'It's weird, I've only known you for a couple of hours, but I've never felt happier. It's as if we've known each other for eternity.'

She smiled. It was almost time. She had him. Not long now, not long to go. 'Eat your food before it gets cold. We can talk more later. We've got all the time in the world.'

They ate in virtual silence for the next five minutes or so, as Harry indulged erotic fantasies of future carnal delights, and Achara considered her next move in line with her training.

Her earlier anxieties had dissipated, and she was beginning to think she may not need to use the drug at all. 'Use your feminine wiles to your advantage.' That's what her lead instructor had said more than once in that oh so insistent way of hers. 'Play to your obvious strengths. If you're targeting a man, flirt with him, flutter your eyelids, stick your boobs out and pout suggestively. Men are simple, so predictable, so easy to manipulate. You'll have him eating out of the palm of your hand in no time at all.' Achara had laughed at the time, doubting the sense of it all as she'd sat and listened in the classroom, but it was all beginning to make absolute sense now that she could witness the results for herself. She could hear the instructor's voice in her head as if she were there now in the room. 'You're a pretty girl, Achara. Flatter his ego, and he'll be putty in your hands.' And it seemed the teacher had had it spot on. This poor boy was so desperate to please. So ready to forget his grief and move on to another relationship with a virtual stranger. Men were such limited creatures. Except for the master, of course. That went without saying. Poor Harry was like a puppy begging for his next treat. Driven by the hormone-fuelled desires of youth.

'Do you fancy another banana shake, Harry?'

He shook his head with a smile, resting his hands on his lap. 'No, I'm good thanks. Nice, though. I really like this place.'

Achara checked the wall clock to her right. It was too soon to leave. Another twenty minutes would be just about perfect. She had to time it exactly right. Nothing less was acceptable. Not if she was to impress her superiors and win favour. She met Harry's tear-stained eyes and smiled warmly, revealing perfect white teeth that gleamed. 'I'm going to order a peppermint tea to finish off our meal. It aids digestion. Why don't you join me? You wouldn't be sorry. It's a lot better for you than the beer you seem to like so much.'

Harry grinned, shifting in his seat. 'I've never tried it.'

Achara waved to the same attentive waitress. 'Well, now's your chance. You're not in any rush, are you?'

Harry shook his head. 'No, not in the slightest.'

'Well, that settles it. I'll order us a pot for two.'

Achara agitated the fresh mint for a full two minutes before pouring. 'I think it's time you told me a bit more about yourself.'

'I'm just a student, like I said. I don't know how much there is to tell.'

She tilted her head at a slight angle. 'Oh, come on, don't put yourself down. You must have lots of interesting facts to share.'

'Such as?'

'Well, you can tell me where you live for a start.'

Harry sipped his tea, grimacing as the hot liquid burned his tongue. 'I err, I share a house with a couple of mates on the same course. It's up near to the university in Curzon Street. It's a bit of a dump, to be honest, but the location is convenient.'

'That sounds ideal.'

Harry laughed. 'I couldn't afford anywhere better even if I wanted to. You know what us student types are like, drowning in debt. What about you?'

Achara paused before responding, breathing deeply, wanting to present as relaxed a persona as possible. She was eager not to put him on his guard but feared she may. This was it, deep breaths, Achara. The time had come. 'I'm a member of a small and friendly community living in a lovely woodland area about five miles from Llandeilo.'

Harry visibly stiffened, unwelcome questions bombarding his mind. 'A community?'

'Yes, that's right, I've been a member since I was sixteen. Mum visited her sister in Thailand and never came back. Dad wasn't an easy man to live with. I was scared. My life had fallen apart. But then I met someone from the community in a Cardiff café, a bit like this one. I visited and realised it was meant to be. I had a new family. The family I was supposed to be with all along.'

Harry raised a hand to touch his face. 'I hope you don't mind me asking, is it some kind of religious thing or something?'

She felt for the glass vial in her pocket, touching it with the fingers of her right hand, regretting her frankness, thinking for the first time that success may not prove as easy as she'd thought. 'No, not at all, it's nothing like that. We're just a group of people with similar tastes and opinions, who try to live sustainably with a low carbon footprint, looking after mother earth to the benefit of us all. We build from wood, make our own clothes, grow our own food, all organic, and contribute as we can, that sort of thing. We're trying to create a better world. There's no religious element. Or at least none that you need to worry about. I don't know why you'd think there was.'

Harry struggled for a response, suspecting she had some unspoken ulterior motive in befriending him, but not wanting to believe it. Was he being recruited, evangelised? *Oh, for fuck's sake, is that what's happening here?* It seemed a distinct possibility. 'It's just something that came to mind, that's all. I didn't mean anything by it. I'd like to know more. What sort of people live there?'

Achara asked herself how much to share. 'Oh, there are artists, writers, poets, musicians, carpenters, gardeners, electricians, people from all walks of life with a wide range of skills. We support each other as best we can, live as we choose and get together to socialise and celebrate on special occasions. I've never felt more fulfilled or more at peace. All humans should live the way we do. The world would be a better place if they did.'

Harry ran a finger around the brim of his teacup. Maybe it wasn't a religious thing at all. He wanted to believe it. He was desperate to believe it. But he still had his doubts. Nagging doubts that wouldn't let go. 'Ah, okay, that all sounds interesting.'

Achara studied Harry carefully, pondering her next move, weighing up her options. He sounded less than convinced. The atmosphere had changed. There was a definite tension in the air despite her best efforts. She so wanted to tell him about the master. To expound his heroic virtues and supernatural powers, but how could this boy even begin to comprehend the master's majesty? How could anyone understand his otherworldly gifts without experiencing them for themselves? Such things were beyond mere human comprehension. 'I'm pleased you find my lifestyle interesting. That's something we share.'

Harry pressed his lips together. 'Look, I've got to ask. Are you certain it's not a religious thing? I'd rather know now if it is. My aunt's heavily involved with a local church. It's the most important thing in her life. It has been since she left school from what my mother's told me. Each to their own, but it's not for me.'

'I've already told you all there is to say. Why don't you come and visit? I could introduce you to my friends, show you around. You could see the place for yourself. What do you think? We can go today if you'd like?'

What to say? What the hell to say? 'I'd really like to see you again, but I'm not quite ready for the whole community thing. Maybe another time when we've got to know each other a little better. How about we arrange to meet up later in the week for a drink or a bite to eat? Or there's a film I'd quite like to see in the local cinema if you're up for it? My treat next time.'

Achara rechecked the clock, glancing surreptitiously and quickly looking away. 'I noticed some leaflets advertising an art exhibition on the small table next to the door. Do you mind getting me one? I meant to pick one up when we came in.'

Harry rose to his feet, a quickly vanishing smile on his boyish face. He manoeuvred past her, bowing in mock courtesy, body lowered, knees bent, keen to make her smile. 'Your wish is my command, my lady.'

Achara took the small glass vial from her trouser pocket and clutched it tightly in one hand, as she looked up and watched him walk away. She unscrewed the black plastic top below the table with trembling fingers, dropped it, and picked it up again. She glanced around the room in search of non-existent prying eyes, as Harry began sifting through various bright leaflets in search of the one she wanted. Achara looked from table to table, still on full alert, but satisfied with her subterfuge, biding her time. The lunchtime rush was over – the few remaining customers seemed focussed on other things, eating, chatting, drinking, uninterested and unaware of her activities. It was now or never. The time had come. This was her one and only opportunity to impress her superiors, and she had to take it. Letting the boy slip away wasn't an option she was willing to entertain, not for a single moment.

Achara moved her cup aside and poured the clear liquid into Harry's tea before quickly returning the empty vial to her pocket along with its top. She sat back in her comfortable seat, controlling her breathing, trying to look as unfazed as possible as Harry returned to the table with leaflet in hand. 'Does it look interesting?' she asked, working to keep her voice from quivering.

He sat next to her, moving up close. 'Yeah, I'd say so. It's an end-of-term thing at the art college near the university next Friday evening, if you fancy it? We could go together. What do you think? I'm up for it if you are.'

Achara knew that he had a very different destiny, a better future if he met the required standards of the community, but she smiled warmly, nodding, nonetheless. 'That would be nice.' She reached out, touching his hand, stroking it tenderly. 'Drink your tea. It's not going to stay warm forever. It would be a shame to waste it.'

Harry hadn't particularly enjoyed the minty taste, but he was keen to please. He raised the cup to his mouth, head back, Adam's apple protruding, emptying it in one generous gulp before placing it back on the table.

'Someone's thirsty!'

He adjusted his position, nudging up, settling himself next to her on the settee so that their thighs were touching. 'Why don't you tell me more about this community of yours? Where is it exactly?'

Achara shook her head slowly, raising a slender finger to her closed lips and holding it there for a second. 'Oh, that's a secret, we like to keep it exclusive, but I may show you, if you're lucky. I'm sure you'd love it as much as I do.'

Harry stretched, yawning as the fast-acting sedative began to take effect. 'Yeah, maybe I'll visit one day.'

The Student

Achara studied him closely. 'How are you feeling, Harry? You're looking a little tired. Is everything okay?'

Harry closed his heavy eyes for a second or two before forcing them open, shaking his head to clear it as the room became an impressionist blur. 'I'm, err, I'm feeling a bit weird. I was fine a few minutes ago. I don't know what the hell's wrong with me.'

She looked deep into his eyes, interested, studying the effects of the drug on his system. 'You said you feel strange, but strange how?'

Harry opened his mouth wide, yawning again at full volume. 'Um... I feel, err, light-headed, dizzy... I'm losing focus. I'm feeling like shit. It's scaring me, to be honest. It's not like anything I've experienced before.'

Achara stood, looking down at him, placing an open hand on his shoulder. 'Maybe it's the alcohol. It seems the most likely explanation. Alcohol's a poison of sorts. And now it's in your system. Maybe your liver can't deal with it.'

Harry shook his head, eyes flickering. 'No, that doesn't make a lot of sense. I only had... had a couple.'

She was quick to reply, rushing her words, her tone raising an octave. 'Yes, that's true, but you drank on an empty stomach. That's never a good idea. You have to admit I'm right. Look at the state you're in.'

Harry slumped to one side, drifting close to unconsciousness as Achara took his arm. She shook him, gently at first, and then more vigorously when he didn't respond nearly quickly enough for her liking. 'Come on, Harry, up you get. Let's take you outside into the fresh air. The oxygen will do you good. It will help clear your head. Come on, you'll be feeling better before you know it.'

He lifted himself upright with the aid of the tabletop, swaying to right and left as he stood. He looked like his leaden legs could give way under him at any moment. 'My head's banging. I'm scared, Achara. Something's not right. What the hell's happening to me?'

Achara placed three ten-pound notes on the countertop and guided Harry towards the door one unsteady step at a time.

'I think I need a d-doctor. Maybe you should c-call an am-ambulance.'

She opened the café door, and led him out into the afternoon sunshine, humming a familiar tune she'd come to love. 'Come on, Harry, keep moving, that's it, one step at a time. My car's parked at the other end of town. You've got to make an effort. I'll look after you. Don't you worry about a thing.'

He stumbled and almost fell as she held him upright. 'I think I need to go to c-casualty. I'm ill, Achara, I'm r-really ill. I really am feeling like crap.'

She supported his weight, manoeuvring him down the meandering lane in the direction of the main street. 'Try not to worry. That's it, open your eyes, one step at a time. You're in good hands. Just trust me. I'm going to make sure you get all the help you need. Do everything I tell you, that's the important thing. Follow my instructions to the letter, and you'll be absolutely fine.'

5

The big man glared at Achara, leaving her in no doubt as to his displeasure as she struggled towards the van, every muscle and sinew screaming for attention with the effort of it all.

'You're twenty minutes late, girl! Where the hell have you been?' There was a hard edge to Baptist's voice that left Achara shuddering.

'I'm so sorry, Baptist. I've done my best. He's half asleep. Look at the state he's in. I only just managed to get him here at all.'

Baptist scowled, a clenched jaw changing the contours of his face. 'How much did you give him?'

Achara avoided the big man's eyes, focussing on the pavement at her feet. 'The whole bottle.'

Baptist ground his teeth together, snarling, his face contorting. 'Oh, for goodness sake, girl! Half the bottle, that's what you were told. Give the target half the bottle initially, assess the results, and then a further dose if required. Your instructions couldn't have been clearer!'

'I'm sorry.'

'Look at him! He only weighs about ten stone dripping wet. You should have known better. You've been told the correct protocol often enough. Didn't you listen? You're lucky he didn't collapse and die.'

She was weeping now, panting, her chest heaving as she gasped for breath. 'I'm sorry, I'm really sorry. What more can I say?'

Baptist shook his head dismissively, unwilling to let it go. 'Half the bottle would have been more than enough for optimum results. It's a simple enough system. What part of that didn't you understand?'

Achara struggled to guide Harry towards the van's rear doors, which were already open. She stumbled on determinedly, one step, two steps, but then lost her footing, hitting the pavement hard. She found herself down on the ground with Harry lying next to her, moaning incoherently as blood seeped from the back of his head where it had cracked against the kerbstone.

Baptist rushed towards them in two easy bounds. He reached down, dragged Harry to his feet with one hand, and placed him over a muscular shoulder with consummate ease. The big man resisted the impulse to swear as several weekend shoppers stopped mid-step, looking in their direction. Baptist looked at each of them in turn, meeting their eyes, shouting out above the noise of the busy street to make himself heard. 'The idiot boy's drunk! It's his eighteenth birthday. Move on, there's nothing to see here. Mind your own business and get on with your lives.'

Baptist lowered Harry into the back of the van as the majority of onlookers lost interest, walking off in the direction of one shop or another, the brief interlude over. He pushed the doors closed and secured them, turning to Achara, who was sitting on the warm pavement, massaging a grazed knee in a flood of tears that wouldn't let up.

'For goodness sake, get up, girl. On your feet and in the van. Today's been enough of a disaster already without you falling apart like some helpless child at the worst possible time.'

Achara rose slowly to her feet, still exhausted, still dazed.

'Hurry up, girl! Do you really want to let the master down after all he's done for you? Stop feeling sorry for yourself, pull yourself together and focus on the bigger picture.'

Achara glanced down at her bloodstained, torn cotton trousers, suddenly on full alert as her heartbeat gradually stabilised. She jumped into the van, sliding along the worn seat and picturing Harry, lost in a deep, drug-induced sleep that would last for hours.

Achara stared at the side of the big man's head as he settled himself into the driver's seat with the second young woman immediately next to him. 'Please don't tell the master what's happened here today. I'll do anything, anything you want. I'm begging you, Baptist. I've seen you looking at me. I know you like me.' And then a line she'd used before. 'Help me, and I'll give you the best time of your life.'

Baptist started the old diesel engine with the second turn of the key. He checked his rear-view mirrors and manoeuvred out into the intermittent traffic with a look of continuing concern etched on his heavily lined face. He was in no rush to reply. In no hurry to ease her angst. When he finally spoke, there was a hard edge to his voice that made Achara shudder. 'The master knows everything. He sees all. Don't ever forget that. And as for your feeble attempts to manipulate me, it might be an idea to remember that sexual congress is only possible with the master's express permission. What were you thinking, girl? Have you learnt nothing on your path to wisdom? Integrity is everything. You shouldn't ever make promises you're not in a position to keep, not to any member of the community. That's the rule.'

Achara looked down, feeling as if her insides were quivering. 'Will you tell him? Please don't tell him. I'll do better next time. It was just a simple mistake, no more than that. I panicked, and I gave the target too much of the sleeping draft. I recognise my failings. That's an error I'll never make again. I've learnt a hard lesson. That's a positive, isn't it? Can't we leave it at that?'

The big man paused before responding, making her wait again. 'Do you really think you deserve another opportunity after all the problems you've caused?'

Achara wiped away her tears. 'I got him here, didn't I?' She pointed behind her. 'He's right there in the back. The process wasn't a complete disaster.'

Baptist blew a long breath from his mouth. 'I hope you're not trying to justify your incompetence. You drew attention to us. People were staring, and that's never a good thing. We need to keep a low profile. What part of that don't you understand?'

She shook her head, thinking before speaking. 'I'm sorry, Baptist, I'm truly sorry. What more can I say?'

Baptist pressed down on the horn, shaking a clenched fist as a car crossed lanes a little too close to the van for his liking. He feared Achara's failings would be seen as his failings. That's how things worked out sometimes within the hierarchy. Others had made that mistake at their cost. 'I'll only discuss your shortcomings with the master if he raises the issue himself. He's got far more important things to think about. We've got the boy, as you say. The day hasn't been a complete failure despite your best efforts. Hopefully, that will be enough.'

Achara's relief was evident. She sucked the warm summer air deep into her lungs, releasing it slowly through pursed lips as she tried to relax, head bowed, her shoulders slumped over her chest. 'Thank you, Baptist. Thank you so very much. I owe you. I won't forget this. Your mercy is truly appreciated. I'm humbled by your generosity of spirit.'

He changed down the gears, engaging neutral as the traffic slowed almost to a stop. 'Don't ever let it happen again, that's all I'm saying.'

The second girl swivelled in her seat, reaching out to squeeze Achara's arm in silent support as Baptist glanced in the driver's side-wing mirror, scowling.

Achara pushed up one leg of her cotton trousers, observing the dark blood still seeping from her wound. It had almost stopped. It wasn't anything to worry about. Nothing serious, just a bit of a cut that would heal up soon enough with God's help.

Baptist approached a roundabout on the outskirts of town, taking the second exit in the direction of Swansea, pressing the accelerator to the floor as the speed limit increased to seventy. 'I don't want any more blood on the seat, it stains. The van needs to be as close to immaculate as possible before the master sees it again. He's got more than enough to concern him without the negative consequences of your ineptitude. Have I made myself clear?'

Achara hung her head. She was very close to panic now, lost in a sea of despair as a more senior position in the community became a distant hope in her increasingly troubled mind. She struggled for the right words. Anything that may satisfy him even slightly. 'My leg's still bleeding, but what can I do?'

'Think of something!'

She took off her white cotton T-shirt, folding it once, then again, before pressing it to her wound, holding it tight. She swallowed before speaking, keen to change the subject. 'Which way are we going to go today?'

Baptist glanced in the rear-view mirror for a second time and smiled. 'We'll continue down the M4 as far as Cross Hands and then double back via Ammanford before heading towards Llandeilo and on from there. I've used the route before, but not for several months. It shouldn't be a problem if we keep a low profile. There aren't any cameras once we're off the motorway.'

Achara nodded, adjusting her bra, picturing Harry's sleeping form, recalling the slight movement of his chest and starting to worry. 'The boy will wake up, won't he, Baptist? I know I gave him too much. It was stupid, foolish. He seems like a nice enough lad for an uninitiated. It would be such a shame if he died. I'm sure he could be put to good use with the right training.'

'If he wakes up, he wakes up, and if he doesn't, well, it's God's will. Such things are beyond our control as mere mortals. You have to learn to accept that. He wouldn't be the first to die. Such things are sent to try us, our cross to bear. Light comes from darkness. We'd just have to dispose of the body. It's as simple as that.'

Achara closed her eyes for a beat, silently admonishing herself, thinking the question ill-judged. How could she let herself down so very badly? She still had so much to learn. She touched her leg, avoiding her injury, and then ran her slender fingers through her hair. 'The master could perform a miracle, couldn't he, if he chose to? If he thought it was the right thing to do. Nothing is beyond his abilities. You told me that. He's capable of anything.'

Baptist increased his white-knuckle grip on the steering wheel, yelling at full volume. 'I wonder what goes on in that head of yours sometimes, girl. Would you really want to trouble the master with the negative consequences of your ineptitude? Have you ever considered the potential consequences for you as the pupil? Or for me as your mentor, for that matter. It wouldn't go well for either of us. That I can promise you. There would be an inevitable price to pay. Actions have consequences. It's the way of the universe. You know I speak the truth.'

Achara bit her lower lip hard, tasting blood. 'I'm really sorry, I didn't think.'

He punched the dashboard repeatedly with a clenched fist, eyes bulging as his rage intensified. 'No, you didn't.' There was a mix of anxiety and anger in his voice as he continued, hissing his words, spitting them from his mouth. 'I strongly suggest you shut your foolish mouth until we get back to the compound. Is that clear enough for you? Do you think you can manage that much without cocking up again? Is that within your gift?'

Achara pictured the master's disapproving face in her mind's eye, and slowly dissolved into a flood of tears which became a full-blown torrent as her chest heaved. 'Yes, Baptist, anything you say.'

'Shut up, girl!'

'I'm s-sorry.'

He was red in the face now, angrier than she'd ever seen him as his blood pressure soared to a savage high. 'Which part of "shut up" didn't you understand? Am I not speaking English? Am I not projecting my words clearly enough for your oriental ears?'

Achara briefly considered another apology, or an objection, maybe an objection, but no, what was she thinking? Sometimes it was best to say nothing at all. She pressed herself into her seat, shoulders hunched, chin resting on her chest, making herself smaller. She sat there fighting back her tears, silently repeating a favoured community mantra in her head time and again as a source of comfort. And the more she repeated it, the better she felt. Her feelings of dread were slowly replaced by a sense of internal peace as the outside world faded away almost to nothing. Achara continued her meditation as Baptist sped through the west Wales countryside, rolling green fields on every side as far as the eye could see. But her eyes were closed tight shut. She was entirely oblivious to nature's beauty. The blue sky, the white cotton wool clouds and the multicoloured wildflowers didn't exist for her. Only the words mattered. Only the veneration she felt for the man she considered a living god. Achara smiled as her high, sweet voice became louder in her mind, drowning out her capacity for reasoned thought. *God is great. I am nothing. All praise to the master. God is great. I am nothing. All praise to the master!*

6

Probationary Police Constable Tanya Evans followed the aged white van for almost five miles before finally deciding to pull it over. Police work was still relatively new to her and putting on the blue lights still held an element of excitement that pleased her a little more than it probably should. A faulty exhaust was hardly the most serious offence in the world, but it had been an unusually quiet day. Anything to break the mind-numbing monotony would provide a welcome interlude. That was all the excuse she needed. Why not have a quick word with the driver before heading back to the station for a bite to eat and a bit of paperwork? It couldn't be put off forever, however tempting. She was a people person. A social animal who thrived on human interaction. Form-filling was a part of the job she hated.

The young officer flicked the signal lever, switched on the blue lights, and steered the patrol car into the adjacent lane. She pressed her foot down hard on the accelerator, engine revving to maximum, overtaking the target vehicle at speed before hitting the brake, slowing, and coming to a final stop in the hard shoulder. She still found such things exhilarating, and as she pulled up the handbrake and switched off the engine, she was very much hoping the novelty wouldn't wear off anytime soon. She'd always been a speed freak, and it was still a lot of fun.

Baptist looked back, sweating, deep in thought. He asked himself if he should drive off at speed when the interfering pig exited the patrol car. But was that sensible? He weighed up his limited options, his head feeling as if it may explode. The pressure was building in his mind, booming compression and sound making him squirm as he struggled to reach a resolution that was even remotely acceptable. He could try to lose the bitch. It was worth considering. But no, that was never going to work, not with the limits of the old diesel engine. *Damn it! Inaction isn't an option. I have to do something.*

Baptist braked hard; the decision made. He pulled up about twenty yards or so behind the police car, fighting the impulse to scream out his frustration as the blue-uniformed officer exited the vehicle and began ambling towards them. Baptist cursed every breath the officer took as he turned stiffly in his seat, moving his entire upper torso as opposed to his head. He glared at the two young women, speaking with urgency, his escalating anxiety clearly etched on his bearded face. 'Do everything I tell you to do and do it quickly. If the bitch looks in the back, we are screwed. And keep your mouths tight shut. Leave the talking to me. Try to relax and put on a good performance. She's getting nearer.' He was yelling now, irate. 'Right, this is it, she's almost here. This has to be convincing.'

Baptist could feel beads of cold sweat forming on his brow as he glanced back again, watching with mounting concern as the officer approached the driver's door. He forced a less than convincing smile, meeting the constable's quizzical gaze, ignoring the inclination to look away as his headache escalated still further. He wanted to hit out. He wanted to pound her to the ground for daring to interfere in God's holy work. But cars were passing, drivers snooping, passengers watching, sticking their noses in where they didn't belong. Violence wasn't an option, however justified. He had to play the game.

'What can I do for you, officer? I don't think I was speeding.'

PC Evans looked first at the driver, and then at the two young women sitting next to him. She couldn't put her finger on what it was exactly, but there was something about the scene that didn't feel right. Call it copper's intuition, a gut feeling. There was definitely something. 'I don't know if you're aware of the problem, but I could see clouds of dark fumes pouring from your exhaust as I followed you along the road. It's excessive, it's obviously faulty and it's an environmental hazard. You need to sort it out.'

Baptist's headache lifted slightly. The pig bitch didn't suspect a thing. 'Ah, yes, sorry, it's something I've been meaning to sort out.'

'A faulty exhaust is an offence under the Road Traffic Act. You need to get it repaired as soon as practically possible.'

Baptist repeatedly nodded, gaining in confidence, sensing her inexperience but still seeking to appear as conciliatory as possible. 'I'll get it sorted as a matter of urgency, guaranteed. I give you my word. Thank you for pointing it out, it's appreciated.'

'I'd like to see your driver's licence, MOT certificate, and insurance documents, please.'

Baptist made a show of searching the glove box for the non-existent paperwork. 'Oh, shit, I felt sure I had them with me. I must have left them back at the house. Sod's law, eh? Sorry about that.'

'Where's that, exactly? The house, where do you live?'

He cleared his throat. 'We travelled from Cornwall for the music festival in Laugharne a couple of days back. We're thinking of staying in the area for a bit longer before heading back to the West Country. It's a lovely area, and the people are friendly enough. So we thought, why not make the most of it?'

'Any good, the festival, any good?'

He nodded, hoping she wouldn't ask any questions he couldn't answer. 'Yeah, brilliant, we'll come again. You should try it yourself. It's not quite Glastonbury, but it's well worth a visit. And it can only get better with time.'

Evans took a small beige booklet of forms and a clear plastic biro from a pocket. 'Is the vehicle registered in your name, sir?'

Baptist claimed it was, speaking with apparent assurance, as his passengers sat in nervous silence. His confidence was slowly slipping away. The pig seemed more determined than he'd expected. What if she checked the computer records? Did she suspect something? The bitch was asking too many questions. Maybe he should resort to violence after all.

'Full name and address, please.'

Baptist shifted uneasily in his seat. He'd role-played this exact situation more than once, the interfering authorities sticking their snouts in. *Think man, think.*

The officer tensed, the tiny hairs on her arms standing to attention, pressing against her shirt sleeves. 'Is there a problem, sir?'

'Sorry, I was thinking about the concert... it's Paul, Paul Thomas, yeah, Paul Thomas. We didn't get a lot of sleep last night. It seems I'm not thinking straight. I didn't mean to mess you about. That's the last thing I'd want.'

Evans studied him closely. 'And the address?'

Baptist was quick to respond this time, providing false information without hesitation, as Evans recorded his reply in her pocketbook in barely decipherable black script.

'I'm going to issue you with a HORT1, Mr Thomas. You'll need to produce your documents at a police station of your choice within five days.'

The tension evaporated from the big man's face. 'Is that something I can do when we're back in Cornwall?'

Evans finished writing and then tore the form from the booklet and handed it to him. 'Yes, as I said, any police station of your choice. But please ensure you do it before the deadline expires. A failure to do so could result in prosecution.'

Baptist grinned, his concerns melting away. 'That's no problem, it's no problem at all. I'll make sure I get it done... is it okay if we continue our journey? It's our first time in this part of the world. We need to find somewhere suitable to stay before everywhere gets fully booked. We're looking for a campsite, that sort of thing. Somewhere we can park the van for the night, ideally with a shower block and toilets. Any recommendations?'

The officer peered into the vehicle, asking herself why one of the two young women was only wearing a bra and loose cotton trousers, one leg of which appeared to be bloodstained. It was warm, for sure, but why no top? It didn't make a lot of sense. And why the blood? 'Is everything all right, girls? You look a little tense, if you don't mind me saying so.'

Both young women replied in the affirmative, forcing improbable smiles that looked strangely out of place.

Evans met Achara's eyes. 'I have to ask. It's warm but not particularly hot. Why haven't you got a top on? Why just the bra?'

Achara pointed to her knee before responding. 'I fell and spilt a drink over myself. I'm waiting for my blouse to dry. Not that it's any of your business.'

The officer's face reddened. 'As long as you're both certain you're okay?'

Achara's gut churned and twisted as she imagined Harry waking and calling for help. She resisted the inclination to look back, anywhere but back, even though there was nothing to see. She replied for both of them. 'Yes, yes, we're absolutely fine, thanks. The sun is out, the birds are singing. All is right with the world.'

The officer glanced from one young woman to the other, thinking the statement a little odd. Maybe it was a hippy thing. 'Okay, if you're both sure.'

Both female passengers smiled, nodding reassuringly as Baptist tapped a finger on the steering wheel. He restarted the tired engine on the third turn of the key, praying under his breath until it finally fired into reluctant life. He looked at Evans for one last time. 'If that's everything, officer, we'll make a move.'

'What's in the back?'

Baptist tensed, struggling to come up with an adequate reply right up to the time the officer's radio crackled into life.

'Control to PC 182, come in please.'

Evans held the radio to her face. 'Yes, what is it, sarge?'

'Where are you, Tanya?'

'I'm on the M4, near Cross Hands.'

'Get back to the station. I need a lift.'

'What, now?'

'Yeah, as soon as you can.'

Evans turned to Baptist, who was mouthing a prayer of thanks. 'That will be all for today, sir. You can be on your way.'

7

When Harry first opened his eyes almost twelve hours later, he thought for one glorious but all too brief moment that his new reality was just a dream, a creation of his subconscious mind. But as his head began to pound, he realised that his unfamiliar surroundings were all too real.

He lifted both hands to his aching scalp, his heart seemingly thumping in his throat as he glanced around the large, rectangular room, with its dark, stained wooden walls and rows of identical single beds covered with grey, perfectly folded blankets. Harry searched for his phone with quick moving fingers, delving into one pocket and then another. To his anguish, it was lost. Without his phone it was impossible to tell what time it was, and he had no idea how long he'd been asleep. He'd certainly missed taking two pills though, one before bed and one at breakfast. The doctor had warned him not to miss doses, and to not try stopping or changing the regime without supervision.

Harry struggled to his feet, keen to make sense of his new surroundings. He approached one of three large metal-barred windows. It had a clear view of what looked like a deserted military parade ground or prison exercise yard, encircled with other wooden structures and mature woodland that appeared to screen the entire area.

He stared out, partially hidden, fearful of being seen, trying to fathom the unfathomable. Where the hell was he? And how the fuck had he got there? Was he really that pissed that he couldn't remember a thing? Surely not, he'd only had a couple of pints. It wasn't the first time he'd drunk when taking medication and the interaction between his antidepressants and alcohol had never knocked him out like that before. *What the fuck? It makes no sense at all.*

Harry turned away from the window, calling out Achara's name, once, then again, louder this time, but all was silence. A strange pervasive silence that demoralised him still further as his eyes darted from one corner of the room to another. He swallowed twice, grimacing as a mouthful of acidic vomit rose in this throat, making him gag. And then those same unanswered questions that wouldn't let up.

Where am I? Where the hell am I? Think, Harry, think! He cast his mind back to the events of the previous day, searching his mind, taking it all in. He could clearly remember meeting Achara, beautiful, lovely Achara with her seductive good looks and unusual but friendly persona. He could recall going to the vegetarian café, the friendly chatter, a tasty meal, milkshake, and then nothing, absolutely nothing. It wasn't like the vague fog of alcoholic excess he'd experienced in the past. It was more than that, much more. The hours between then and now seemed a total blank, a vacuum, as if he hadn't existed for a time.

Harry touched the back of his head, wincing on finding a scab. He attempted to recall the cause of the injury, but without success. He looked urgently to his right and flinched as a wall-mounted camera secured high in one corner of the room suddenly buzzed into eager life, following his every move as he rushed to right and left, scanning the wooden floorboards in search of his phone. And then a voice, a disembodied, high-pitched female voice with a strong accent he couldn't identify, spoke out from each of four unseen speakers implanted in the ceiling, clearly enunciating each word in sharp tones that couldn't fail to get his attention.

'Hello, Harry, I hope you're well rested. It's my great honour to welcome you to our small community. You are here as a guest of the master. Try to relax. You will be provided with suitable refreshments as soon as you've made your bed to the required standard and have dressed appropriately. Just look at the other beds, and you'll understand what you need to do. You're truly blessed to have this opportunity. I strongly advise you to ask for God's help to take full advantage. You're one of the lucky ones. Not everyone will survive the coming storm. We are God's chosen people. You are blessed, my brother. Welcome!'

Harry was visibly shivering now, not from cold – he was hot and sweating – but due to the residual effects of the drug and a situation he found impossible to compute or comprehend. He searched frantically for his phone, acutely aware of his vulnerability as silence prevailed once more. But all he found was a white cotton T-shirt, matching cotton trousers and flip-flops, much like those worn by Achara the previous day. For a moment Harry hoped the clothes may be hers, that she'd suddenly appear to alleviate his growing dread. But as he held the trousers up in front of him in the light of a window, he realised they were far too big for her slight frame and intended for him. He made one last urgent search for his smartphone, lowering himself to the wooden floorboards and looking under the many beds, but without success. It was time to get out of there. Time to get back to normality. It really was as simple as that.

Harry rushed towards the room's only door, which wouldn't open, however hard he tried. He turned the metal handle as far as it would go, forcing it down, using all his limited weight and strength to pull the door towards him in the forlorn hope that it was merely stiff rather than locked. He threw his shoulder against it and when it didn't budge an inch, he went stumbling backwards, a sharp jolt of pain firing down one arm and making him shudder.

He hurried towards each of the three windows in turn, pulling ineffectively at the steel bars with increasing urgency as others had before him, but to no effect at all. If someone didn't let him out of there, he wasn't going anywhere. What the hell was going on? The entire structure seemed secure, a prison of sorts. A wood and steel enclosure that penned him in.

Harry was sweating profusely now. He sucked the warm summer air deep into his lungs as the metal click of a key in the lock made him jerk his head back and stare. He focussed on the door with a heady mix of anticipation and apprehension, as it was opened by a large, overly muscular man of six foot four or five inches, dressed in those same white clothes. He was carrying a copper-coloured tray laden with a white ceramic bowl of what Harry assumed must be food, and a tall glass of water.

Harry took a backward step as the huge man's imposing bulk filled the entire doorframe, rather than rush towards him as he'd initially intended. He shouted on retreating, adrenaline surging through his system, fight or flight but with nowhere to run. 'What's going on? Where the hell's my phone? You can't keep me here! Please, I just want to go home.'

The big man snorted, chuckling to himself. New initiates invariably acted out their concerns like naughty children in a playground, screaming and shouting, demanding attention, as was their custom. It was nothing new. Nothing he hadn't seen before. 'Sit on the end of your bed, Harry, and listen carefully, there's a good lad. I don't expect to repeat myself. I've got more important things to do with my time.'

Harry had never seen such an impressive individual, not in real life, not up close and personal. He withdrew a little further but remained standing.

'Where's my fucking mobile? You can't keep me here against my will. I want to go home!'

Baptist stared at Harry with unblinking eyes, nostrils flared. He bellowed his words, roaring, 'Sit on the bed, now! Do not make me ask you again. It's my job to ensure your compliance. And it's something I'm good at. Something in which I excel. I'd do what I'm told if I were you. I'm not a patient man.'

Harry wanted to stamp and shout like a petulant child, but instead, he sat as instructed, speaking in a contrived, monotone voice he thought may illicit his desired response without irritating the big man any more than he already had. 'So, where is it?'

'Where's what? Am I supposed to know what you're talking about?'

'My phone, my fucking phone!'

The big man took a step towards him. 'I suggest you modify your language. Profanity is the work of the devil. Words have power. Swearing is not acceptable, not here, not ever. It would serve you well to remember that.'

Harry avoided eye contact. 'Please, can I have my phone? That's all I'm asking, just my phone. There are people I need to contact. People who'll be concerned if they don't hear from me.'

'Initiates are not permitted contact with anyone outside the community until trust is earned. That can take weeks, months or years. You can co-operate or fight God's will and lose. It really is up to you.'

Harry jumped to his feet, throwing his hands up. 'Weeks, months, years! Initiation! For as long as I'm here! What the fuck's all that supposed to mean?'

The big man strolled towards him, casual, still holding the tray out in front of him with one hand while pointing with the other. 'You've been provided with appropriate clothing, food and water. Be grateful for that. You'll discover that a spirit of gratitude benefits you greatly as your initiation progresses. Open your heart and let in the light.'

Harry gripped one wrist, rushing his speech. 'Please, I don't want to be here. I want no part of your initiation. I just want to go home. I need my medication. I can't cope without it. I don't know what else I can say to make you understand.'

'Sit back down, eat your food, and I'll introduce you to the other members of the community later in the day, if, and only if, I think you're ready for that privilege. Advantages are earned rather than given. All will become clear when the time is right. You don't need anything from your old life. Breathe deeply, focus on the breath and calm yourself. This is all very new to you. I understand that and have made allowances accordingly. You have so much to learn.'

Harry splayed his hands out wide. 'I'm a university student, I want no part of your community. I'm not interested. It's not for me.'

'Your old life is at an end, Harry. You've been chosen. You're here as a worker. To help with chores, maintenance, gardening. It's better that you accept that. The universe has decided your fate. Why fight against the inevitable? God is greater than any man. It's not a battle you can win.'

Harry rocked back and forth, tugging his hair, his eyes filling with tears. 'Why the hell aren't you listening to me?'

'You have nothing worthwhile to say.'

'Where's Achara? I want to speak to Achara.'

Baptist sighed, a look of amusement on his face. 'You're nothing if not predictable. Males and females are only permitted to meet with the master's prior consent. That's the rule, that's how it has to be. There are no exceptions, not for you, not for me, not for anyone. The master's word is law here. He converses directly with God.'

'Then ask him! Just fucking well ask him! That's not too much to ask, is it?'

'Swear again, and I'll beat the devil out of you.'

'What?'

'You heard me.'

Harry dropped his head.

'Change your clothes, eat your food, drink your water, and accept your new life with good grace. Be patient, and all will become clear. The master hasn't got time to deal with your mundane trivialities. He's an important man. A busy man sent to save humanity from our many failings and frailties. You'll be given an audience if he considers it appropriate, and not before. It would not be in your interests to ask again.' And then a line he used often. 'I suggest you remember that.'

Harry clenched both hands into tight fists before consciously relaxing them. Fighting wasn't an option. He was a student, an academic, a lover, not a brawler. He had to play to his strengths. The big man may be amenable to persuasion. *Yes, yes, that may do it.* A reasoned approach seemed best. 'Look, I get what you're saying. You're all part of a community that's going to save the world from the coming day of judgement. I understand, I really do. I grew up a Catholic. And your aims are admirable, truly they are. I commend what you're trying to do here, but it's not for me. I'm not worthy. I wouldn't be any good to you at all.'

The big man frowned. 'That's not for you to decide. You've been chosen. Ours is the only true religion. Be glad you can be a part of it before it's too late.'

Harry looked back incredulously. 'I want out of here. I've got a job lined up for the summer. I need to pay the bills. This is mad, totally fucking mad! You can't keep me here against my will. It's against the law, kidnapping. I want to go home.'

'That's not going to happen.'

Harry dropped to his knees. 'Do you want me to beg? Do you want me to fucking beg? Is that it? Because I will if you want me to.'

Baptist approached the bed, setting the tray down as Harry crumbled in front of him. The big man looked down at him with bulging eyes, teeth bared, legs planted wide. 'Swear again, and I'll beat the sin out of you one blow at a time. I find it offensive. God finds it offensive. This is your final opportunity to amend your behaviour. Have I made myself clear?'

'Yes!'

'Yes, what?'

Harry turned away. 'Yes, you've m-made yourself clear.'

'Perfectly clear?'

'Yes, yes, yes!'

'Right, it seems we're finally getting somewhere. Now, get off the floor, sit on the bed, eat your rice, drink your water, change your clothes, and accept your new reality. The past is of no importance, forget it. This is your home now. There is only the now. You'll leave here when the master deems it appropriate, and not before. The rules of the outside world are of no concern to me. The master's word is law.'

Harry sucked in the fetid air, eyes burning bright, fixated on the source of his suffering. Reason seemed lost on the big man. He seemed brainwashed, unmovable, utterly unreasonable in the worst possible way. Harry felt an undeniable surge of anger and frustration rising in every fibre of his being, an unstoppable wave of intense emotion. He jumped off the bed and flung the tray to the floor, attempting to dodge Baptist's flailing arms as he sprinted for the open door. Harry almost made it. As he was about to stride out into the daylight with hopes of escape leaping and dancing in his mind, he was hit by a powerful chest-high tackle that launched him off his feet, sending him crashing to the wooden floor with a sickening thud that left him bruised and battered.

Baptist jumped to his feet in one easy athletic bound. He loomed over Harry, dragging him into an upright position by his hair, tearing a bloody clump from the scalp.

Harry wailed, as the big man grasped his arms with both hands, hurling him back towards his bed with a degree of force that was impossible to resist.

Baptist wasn't even slightly out of breath as he spoke the words that were already becoming all too familiar to Harry's ears. 'Sit yourself down, eat your rice, drink your water, dress appropriately, and accept your new life here. Change is difficult to accept even for the best of us in the most favourable of circumstances. But you'll learn to adapt and grow spiritually given sufficient time, instruction and application. Embrace what our community has to offer you with good grace, and you'll be much better for it. You'll be truly fulfilled for the first time in your life, happier than you've ever been before. Trust in your new destiny, Harry. Free your spirit. That's all you have to do. Try to run again, and it may be the last thing you ever do.'

Harry pressed his palms together, blood seeping from his head wound, staining his face. 'Why, why would you do that to me? I want to go home. Please, I'm begging you. I'm not well. I suffer depression, anxiety. I need my medication. Please, I won't tell anyone what you've done. I just want to go home.'

'Eat your meal, drink your water, and dress appropriately. It will help clear your head. If you need to piss you can use the bowl under the bed. I'll show you the shower and toilet block when you've finished your meal.'

Harry looked around him, attempting to hold back the whimpers and replace them with words. 'My meal? My m-meal?'

Baptist nodded. 'That's what I said.'

'It's all over the floor.' Harry pointed. 'Be reasonable, it's all over the floor!'

'Did I do that?'

Harry struggled to free himself as the big man clutched the front of his sweatshirt, but to no effect. The man was far too large, too muscular, too strong. He dragged Harry to his feet, and repeated himself, noses touching, skin on skin. 'Eat your food like I told you to. And don't get any blood on the floor. Use your top as a bandage. You're not going to be wearing it again.'

'I'm sorry, just let me go, please. I need my tablets. I won't be able to cope without them.'

Baptist threw Harry to the floor, kicking him hard in the ribs a few inches below his armpit, sending him sprawling. 'God is all the medicine you need. If you're ill, it's because you haven't got sufficient faith. You need to understand that your actions have consequences. Now, eat the rice, lap up your water, clean the blood off the floor, get dressed, and make your bed. You've got precisely one hour before I make a full inspection. I want this place immaculate when I come back. If there's even a single grain of rice on the floor or one drop of blood or water, you'll be sorry. Ask for God's help. He has all the strength anyone could require. You don't need your tablets or anything else from your old life. Prayer, hard work and obedience are a cure-all. They give succour to the soul. Have I made myself clear?'

Harry looked up with a pained stare, the skin bunched around startled eyes. 'Yes, yes, a thousand times, yes!'

Baptist stepped on the fingers of Harry's left hand, pressing down hard with gradually increasing force. 'Yes, what?'

Harry shouted out his reply, sobbing. 'Yes, I h-hear you. I hear you!'

The big man pressed down still harder as Harry wailed in

response, and then suddenly lifted his foot. 'Spare the rod and spoil the child. I'm an enthusiastic supporter of that teaching. You'll call me "sir" from here on in. You're utterly worthless until the master deems otherwise. At the very bottom of the heap until that glorious day dawns. That's how the system works here. Got it?'

The throbbing pain from Harry's head and hand were virtually unbearable as he replied in the affirmative. 'Yes, yes, I get it, you're the boss.'

The man mountain held a cupped hand to his ear. 'Yes, what, newbie, yes what? Show me the respect my status deserves.'

'Yes, sir!'

Baptist continued bawling out his commands in the style of a military drill instructor. A strange change of demeanour Harry found impossible to comprehend. As if the big man had two entirely different personalities. Two people wrapped up in the body of one.

'I can't hear you, newbie.'

'Yes, sir!' Louder this time.

'Now, that was much better. I do like a fast learner. Perform your allocated tasks to an acceptable standard, and you *may* avoid getting hurt again. That sounds good, doesn't it, newbie? Just do what you're told and avoid a beating. That shouldn't be too complex a proposition for a clever young student like you to comprehend. You've been keen to demonstrate how clever you are. Now's the time to prove it.'

Harry's face appeared washed-out, pallid, contrastingly stained with slowly congealing blood. He wanted to say something. Anything to appease the man. But he couldn't find the words. His mind was numb, the reality of his situation impossible to understand or accept.

Baptist nudged Harry with a knee, knocking him sideways. 'Now would be a good time to thank me for the guidance I've offered. There's a time for silent meditation, it has its place, but now is not that time.'

'Thank you, sir!'

The big man sniggered as he looked back on approaching the door. 'There you go, you're adapting to your new life already. I told you to eat and drink, now get on with it. Any further punishment you suffer will be down to you. It's a necessity for your own good. Don't let me have to tell you again.'

Harry began crawling about on all fours like a dog in search of nourishment. As he lapped up a small pool of tepid water, he silently acknowledged that he'd never felt so helpless or afraid. They were the kind of intense emotions he'd never felt before, not to that degree, not to such overwhelming extremes that beat him down a little further with every second that passed. He'd been depressed at times, and he'd experienced anxiety too, particularly after the death of his father. But not like this, never like this. It would have been all too easy to crawl into bed and weep, hiding from the world under the covers, as he sometimes had as a child.

He'd created his own private world in those days, not so very long ago. He'd withdrawn into his own mind then, and he could do it now if he were so inclined. But where would that get him? Nowhere, absolutely nowhere. The members of the community must be mad, insane, every single one of them, with their white clothes and confused New Age thinking. Reason wasn't an option. He had to eat. He had to maintain his strength if he was going to get out of there in one piece and return to normality. Escape was his one and only option. Yes, escape and run as fast as his legs could carry him. Faster than he'd ever run before. It was time for action as opposed to thought.

Harry gathered together a small pile of boiled rice with the side of one finger, raising a few grains to his mouth. He sat upright, feeling a little dizzy as he began to chew the unappetising fare, forcing himself to swallow again and again as a single grain stuck in this throat, making him choke. He looked around him, wringing his hands together as the results of prescribed drug withdrawal began to fully kick in. His body ached as badly as if he had flu. He felt exhausted, his muscles hurt, and chills made him shake.

How on earth am I going to cope with such misfortune? Do I have the physical or mental strength to face adversity?

He slumped to the floor, curling up in the foetal position, head down, back curled, and chin tucked into his chest. He saw his dead father's face hovering above him, coming in and out of focus, uttering words of reassurance, urging him to join him in the afterlife, a safe place, free of fear and oppression. Harry reached up as his father's image slowly faded away to nothing. He called out to him, once, then again, but there was no response. It was as if his father had died all over again. As if he was mourning his loss with that same violent emotional intensity he had as a child, before time blunted grief's edges, making it bearable.

Harry raised a hand to his face. He badly needed his pills. How on earth was he going to manage? How could he carry on and survive, let alone thrive? He searched his mind, but he couldn't come up with a satisfactory resolution. Nothing that gave him confidence. Nothing that gave him hope. Events had taken a dramatic turn for the worse. Harry was in no doubt. It was the lowest point of his life.

8

Every room in the large, purpose-built wooden compound was fitted with at least one state-of-the-art, wall-mounted camera, sometimes two, or even three, where the master deemed it necessary or desirable. And that really did mean every room: the communal sleeping quarters, the shower block, and even the toilets.

There was no privacy anywhere for anyone, except for the master himself, who lived in comparative luxury, with ready access to a bank of meticulously maintained colour monitors that enabled him to watch and listen to his subjects every action at will, twenty-four hours a day, seven days a week. Nowhere and nothing was exempt, however personal, however intimate, and the master, or Professor Vincent Cameron, as he'd previously been known, took full advantage when he was in the mood. It was one of his many pleasures. Something he considered his God-given right as the esteemed leader of the community.

His life had changed so very much since he had become leader, and changed for the better. Just as it should be. Just as it was meant to be. That's what he told himself. God had delivered him to eminence. He was unique, exalted, deserving of life's luxuries and indulgences. If not him, then who? The rich man in his castle, the poor man at his gate.

Wasn't that how the hymn went? Yes, yes, of course it was, before some misguided miscreant corrupted the sentiment. They were words of wisdom, an instruction of sorts from on high, a model for life. He was that rich man, and those there to serve him were inconsequential by comparison, whatever their backgrounds or prior achievements. He, and he alone, was at the very pinnacle of God's glorious creation, a living deity, infallible, like no one else on earth.

If others suffered to enhance his life experiences, then so be it. They didn't matter, not in any real sense, not as he did. It was the way of the world, the survival of the fittest. Always had been and always would be. Some were destined for greatness, and he was one of those exalted people.

Everything, Cameron assured himself, *is exactly as it should be. My word is law. And there is nothing wrong with that.*

Cameron relaxed back on his luxurious king-sized bed with a naked young woman to either side of him and pondered the events that had led him to his destiny. It was something he often did, and it pleased and excited him like nothing else could. He took the younger women's right hand in his, placing it directly on his engorged penis before continuing his reminiscences, smiling warmly as his version of events became magnified in his mind.

He hadn't always been a self-proclaimed mystic. No, he'd been a competent and well-respected psychology professor in his previous life. One university lecturer amongst many, deceptively unremarkable until a fortuitously timed television documentary relating to events at The Peoples Temple Agricultural Project, or Jonestown as it was more commonly known, inspired him to create an all-powerful persona that would facilitate his future as a man special amongst men.

It wasn't so much the mass induced suicides of over 900 people that had fascinated him, or at least not the deaths in themselves. It was the cult leader's total domination of his followers' lives he'd found so very attractive and amusing. They'd taken deadly poison and even given it to their children. Wow! That was power, real power, power over life and death. He'd thought about it and had craved that same veneration, that same total dominance over others. He'd been meant to watch the programme. Yes, yes of course he had. He was sure of it. Certain with a degree of vigour that filled him with joy. Some things were meant to be, written in the stars. He'd shouted it out for God to hear, leaving him giddy. It was meant to inspire, designed to provide a vision of the future. What other rational explanation was there? He'd reached the only reasonable conclusion available to him.

It was more than a television programme. More than a fortuitously timed documentary to watch and enjoy. It was a message from on high, meant for him and only him. If Jones could do it, then why not him? That was the key message.

He had all the attributes, the dedication, the understanding, the inclination and intelligence. He'd known his life had changed forever at that precise moment. Bang, just like that. It had hit him between the eyes, never to be forgotten. He was to form a new religion, the one true religion. A faith that would ultimately replace all others. He was sure of it. He'd never been more convinced of anything in his life. He was heading for the very top. A living god! And he was prepared to do almost anything to achieve it.

Cameron beamed as he recalled events and highlighted them in his mind. In the coming months, he'd come up with a plan, a brilliant plan, an inspired project, that reflected his undoubted genius and God's inspiration and intent. He'd created numerous false identities on social media, writing of miracles performed by himself, the great man, the master, the new Messiah, a visionary possessed of infinite possibility and power, who could manifest birds from mid-air, disappear at will, and cure the sick at the mere touch of his hand. And the devotees had flocked to see him, keen to believe, desperate to believe, and oh so ready to hand over a generous donation to thank him and fund his continued work. It had all happened so very quickly in the end. Faster than he could ever have hoped. And now here he was, worshipped, adored, his word was law.

Cameron adjusted his position, grinning as the girl to his left squeezed his penis a little tighter and began moving her hand in a rhythmic motion.

'Does that feel good, master? Does it please you? Your will is my command. I'm here to serve.'

He turned his head to face her. 'Did you know that I established this fine community with my own money? It wasn't all donations. I sold my house in suburbia. A home I'd shared with my disabled mother right up to the time of her death. It was a selfless act of generosity to an undeserving world.'

The young woman continued massaging his penis, up down, up down, bringing him close to climax before responding. 'Yes, master, you told me all about it once before. I'm so very grateful to you. We all are. We're not worthy. You're a truly wonderful man.'

Cameron was panting slightly as he continued expounding his version of events. 'I b-bought the fields, the surrounding w-woodland, and instructed my early followers in building the compound to the exact specifications given to me by God. What do you think of that? Noah had his ark. I have my compound. One day great men will write of my deeds as they did his.'

She slowed her hand. 'That's wonderful, master, please tell us more.'

'God spoke to me, telling me what to do. And I followed his instructions, with few minor adjustments I considered appropriate. Are you impressed by my ingenuity, my children? Because you should be. You really should be. It was a miracle of sorts. I turned a dream to reality in the blink of an eye.'

He groaned on ejaculating, waiting for her inevitable response, as the second young woman began licking his fleshy abdomen.

'You're wonderful, master, truly wonderful. I'm unworthy to serve you. We all are. You're a prince amongst men.'

Cameron suddenly pushed the young woman's head aside a little too roughly, hurting her ear. 'Enough, up you both get. There's a parade in forty minutes. On your way now, get dressed and get out of here. There are important matters I need to address. The responsibilities of leadership are greater and more onerous than you could ever imagine. I need time to prepare.'

Both young women jumped up, keen, alert, speaking in unison, as they had many times before in very similar circumstances. They stood to rigid attention, naked at the end of the bed, heads bowed, worshipping at his feet. 'Yes, master, your word is our command.'

He rose to a sitting position, resting against the headboard. 'I want you both back here this evening at seven o'clock sharp, showered, perfumed and ready for some experimentation. I've got something new in mind. I may even record it on film for posterity. Sex is a gift from God, a blessing. It would be a sin not to indulge our carnal desires to the maximum.'

Sarah, the older of the two women, at twenty-four years old, looked at him with pleading eyes that appeared close to tears. 'Today is my husband's birthday, master, his thirtieth. I was hoping to spend the night with him. It's been several weeks since we've been together. It would mean so very much to him. Do you remember me asking for your permission? You said you'd consider it if I performed to an acceptable standard. Did I not please you sufficiently?'

Cameron glared at her, snarling, spitting his words, as angry as she'd ever seen him, as he shook a fist in the air. 'Are you here to serve your husband? Is that your purpose in life? Think very carefully before you reply. It would not be wise to disappoint me again.'

Sarah drew back, leaning away from him. 'No, master, I'm here to serve you and only you. It's just that I haven't seen my husband for—'

'Who do you serve?'

Sarah dropped to her knees, lowering her head, allowing her long blonde hair to fall across her face. 'I serve you, master. You're my everything, my reason for living. Please forgive my impertinence. I shouldn't even have mentioned it. I spoke out of turn. I still have so much to learn.'

Cameron glared at her for a full thirty seconds or more before finally speaking again, taking his time, enjoying her obvious discomfort. 'Be here on time, and *if* you please me sufficiently, I *may* allow you to spend an hour or two with your husband at some point during the night if I feel so inclined. Will that suffice? Does that meet your needs to a satisfactory level? Speak now or forever hold your peace.'

Sarah smiled warmly, picking up her white cotton clothes, still avoiding his accusing gaze for fear his eyes may penetrate her very soul. 'Thank you so very much, master. You're most generous. I'm unworthy of your kindness and charity. Christopher will be so very pleased when I tell him. He's been looking forward to today. Conjugal visits are still important to him. He hasn't yet adapted as well as I have. I hate to say it, but I think a part of him still hankers after our old life.'

Cameron was wild-eyed as he swivelled on the bed, lowering his feet to the floor. 'Christopher? Who the hell's Christopher?'

Sarah began rocking to and fro, first one way and then the other. 'Lightning, sorry, I err, I meant to call him Lightning. I can only apologise for my stupidity. I won't ever make that mistake again. Christopher no longer exists. He has been reborn with a new name, a new creation.'

Cameron smiled with his eyes, taking her hand in his, satisfied with her slightly garbled response. 'I'll forgive you this one time, my child. God teaches us to be merciful. You can make it up to me later this evening. Try to surprise me. I do so like surprises. Use your imagination. I'm sure you can come up with something special.'

She continued shuffling from one foot to the other. 'Thank you, master. I'm truly blessed to be in your presence. Your kindness overwhelms me.'

'You're very welcome, my child. You all have your weaknesses. I try to make allowances for your lack of wisdom. I don't want to hear another word. Now, run my bath before you go.'

9

Harry watched from a barred window as a gathering of about twenty men, and a much bigger group of women and children of various ages, formed into straight lines on the large, rectangular area of even concrete that formed the central point of the compound. Everyone was dressed in white – white cotton tops, loose white trousers – just like Achara.

All was silence, no one appeared to be talking, not a word, not a whisper, not even the children, which seemed strange and disconcerting. They just stood rigidly to attention about two to three feet apart, with the men in the front row and the women and children behind them, statue-like. As if they were made of stone. As if they weren't living creatures at all.

Harry continued watching for a few minutes more as the gathered members of the community stood in the heat of the day, looking forward with faces that appeared strangely devoid of emotion. Harry was still deep in thought, paralysed by a combination of fear and apprehension when the room's only door suddenly opened. He turned slowly to his right as the same huge, broad-shouldered man entered the room with a distinct air of urgency. As if it really mattered. As if his entrance was the most significant event of the day.

Harry looked on, mouth agape, as Baptist strolled slowly around the room, his hands linked behind him. The big man examined every inch of the clean floor, as Harry pressed himself to the wall, trying to seem as inconspicuous as possible, desperate not to offend or be drawn in. Baptist stopped, glaring at Harry until he quickly looked away.

'Nothing to say for yourself, newbie? You've had plenty of time to think. I saw you peeping through the window a while back, snooping, spying, sticking your beak into other people's business. Surely you must have something to say for yourself. You're not usually so quiet, not with being such a clever intellectual, and all.'

Harry didn't respond. He had other things on his mind, as his bladder threatened to evacuate, soaking the floor where he stood.

'Don't tell me you haven't got any more complaints. No more demands to leave? Come on, tell me what's *really* going on in that pretty little head of yours. I can see the cogs turning. I can see the misgivings etched on your face. Don't think you're fooling anyone. You're as transparent as polished glass.'

Harry shifted his weight from one foot to the other, suppressing his reflexive dance.

'Can I assume that you've concluded that compliance is your best policy? Speak up, newbie. Tell me now. I want to hear you say it.'

Harry nodded twice, glancing at the open door, weighing up his options. Should he make a run for it? Could he make it out into the sunshine before the big man dragged him back? No! He looked away defeated, desperate for his medication, focussing on anything but freedom. 'I've got nothing more to say.'

Baptist stood looking down at Harry's bed for a few seconds before finally shattering the silence. 'Yeah, not bad for a newbie, not bad at all. It seems you've made some effort. That's to your credit. But there's no room for complacency. It's a good start, but that's all it is. You need to keep it up and improve with every hour that passes. We should always seek to better ourselves. We have to operate to our ultimate potential capacity if we're to find enlightenment. In this lifetime, and in all the ones to come, for however long it takes. Nothing less is acceptable. It's the primary purpose of our existence. I want you to take that wisdom on board and embrace it willingly.'

Harry's eyes twitched as he shuffled backwards and forwards, side to side, unable to settle in one place. His escalating anxieties dominated his thinking, his tumbling thoughts were confused and contradictory, fed by a combination of uncertainty and fear. *Should I ask? One last time? It has to be worth a try, doesn't it?* Sprinting for the door again wasn't a viable option. No, not with the big man standing there, not with the bastard blocking his way like a doorman at a weekend nightclub. *Beg, yes beg, just do it, Harry. Make something up, something emotional, something heart-wrenching. Maybe that would work. It had to be worth a try, didn't it?*

'I want to go home, please. I'm an only child. My mother's going to be worried about me. She has serious health problems. She's not at all well. She needs me to look after her. Without me, she has no one.'

'This is your home now.'

Harry swallowed a scream, forcing it back down his throat. 'Then, at least let me ring her. Let me use a phone. Surely that's not too much to ask. She'll be worried sick. I need to let her know I'm alive.'

'Your mother is no longer your concern. We are your family now. You must learn to forget her. She is the past and the community the future. What part of that don't you understand?'

Harry threw his arms up, the whites of his eyes shining, his voice rising in pitch. 'I haven't got any money, if that's what you're thinking. I'm a skint student, my dad died when I was twelve years old, and my mum works as a nurse in a local doctor's surgery. I grew up in a council house, not some posh place full of snobs. If you're thinking about asking for a ransom, you've got no chance. You won't get a penny. My mum's as skint as I am.'

The big man smiled sardonically. 'Do you think we don't know that? God doesn't make mistakes. You're young, you're healthy, and you can gain strength given time. All those are good attributes, useful attributes that can benefit the community as the seasons pass. Others will provide financial resources. We give whatever we can. There is no shortage of generous benefactors. Donations flow to the master's cause.'

'Then, what the hell do you want of me?'

'It seems I need to repeat myself. You're here as a manual worker, gardening, cleaning, painting, and maybe as a novice recruiter at some future date if you show sufficient promise. You'll be provided with suitable training if you're lucky enough to be selected for the programme. You don't need to worry about that. We play to our strengths here, each to their own. Your life has changed forever. None of this has happened by random accident. Everything is just as it should be. Once chosen, there's no going back.'

Harry's face contorted, fear becoming indignant rage as a roller-coaster of emotion left him giddy. 'This is mad, totally fucking mad! It's kidnap, it's fucking kidnap! What the hell is wrong with you? You'll go to prison if you don't let me go. I'll make a statement. I'll give evidence! Everything you're doing to me is against the law.'

Baptist took a slow step towards him, flexing his mighty muscles, driving home his advantage. 'Are you going to co-operate? I just need a yes or a no. But think carefully before answering, newbie. We can do this the easy way or the hard way. And you won't like the hard way. I can promise you that much. Make your mind up. It really is up to you.'

'Co-operate? Co-operate! You abducted me, you mad bastard! I'm being kept a prisoner. Why would I co-operate with you of all people?'

Baptist moved with speed and agility and grabbed Harry by his hair, dragging him towards the open door. Baptist suddenly stopped, jolting Harry back, pinning him to the wall by his throat. He spoke at touching distance, forehead to forehead. 'It seems you're not such a fast learner, after all, newbie. I don't ever want to hear you mention your past life again. Not your mother, not your father, not your happy pills, nothing! This is your home now. All your needs are met. Learn to forget the past, or I'll beat it out of you. Out of kindness, you understand. Everything I do is for your own good. There is little point in grieving the unobtainable.'

Harry was sweating profusely as he looked to left and right, moving just his eyes, still searching for an opportunity to escape, increasingly desperate to regain his freedom. He silently swore that he'd take whatever chance arose, however slight, whenever the time seemed right. He'd grasp his opportunity and run, sprinting away faster than he'd ever run before. It would happen, yes it would definitely happen, but like it or not, as regrettable as it was, now was not that time.

Harry spoke up as Baptist took a backward step. 'I'm sorry, I wasn't thinking. I'll do better. I promise you, I'll do better. This is all so very new to me. So different from what I've experienced in the past. I need time to adapt.'

The big man slammed the door shut behind them, as they stepped outside into the warmth of the day. Baptist appeared suddenly calmer now, less agitated, less irate, but he still spoke with passion, the power of his speech intended to emphasise the importance of his words. 'It's time for you to meet your fellow members of the community. It's a big moment, an important moment. They're your family now. The only people that matter. Everyone else is dead to you. It's time to recognise and accept that reality. It'll be better that way. Why fight the inevitable? Everything that's happening was meant to be. God has a plan for your life.'

Harry nodded frantically, keen to please, buying time, playing the game as he felt he had to. 'Yes, sir, I'm looking forward to meeting them all.'

The big man beamed, his face-stretching smile looking strangely out of place on his craggy face. As if real pleasure was alien to his experience. 'So now you understand?'

'Yes, sir!'

Baptist's smile slowly disappeared to be replaced by a scowl. 'Are you certain of that? God is looking down on us. He wants to hear you say it. There's no room for ambiguity. This is far too important a process for that.'

Harry relaxed his jaw, unwelcome thoughts tumbling in his mind. 'Yes, sir, I understand. You've made yourself perfectly clear. I'm going to do everything I can to adapt.'

Baptist paused, watching Harry closely, studying his expressions and body language with a keen eye born of experience. 'Are you just saying what you think I want to hear, newbie? Is that the reason for your newfound compliance? You wouldn't be the first ingrate to try to pull the wool over my eyes. Is that your little game?'

'No, no, not at all!'

'I hope not, for your sake. That really wouldn't be a good idea. We've got ways of dealing with liars. It wouldn't be a good idea at all.'

Harry shook his head repeatedly, keen to convince his antagonist for fear of punishment. He had never felt more in need of his medication, as self-doubt taunted him, pulling his strings. Was he imagining things, losing his mind? Those piercing blue eyes seemed to look inside him. They seemed to penetrate his very soul. *Say something, Harry, you have to say something.* 'I wouldn't lie to you. I'd never do that. This is all very new to me. Like I said. It's hard to deal with. But I'm doing my best to fit in.'

'Don't ever go thinking you're fooling me, newbie, not for a single second. I know everything you're thinking. I'm not an ordinary man. I'm not like anyone you've ever met before. I've got X-ray vision. I can see inside your head.'

'I wouldn't lie to you. I'd never lie to you.'

Baptist stared at Harry for a few seconds more. He spoke in a hushed whisper, directly into Harry's ear. 'You'd better not be lying, newbie. The master expects the highest standards from all of us, you included. Your word is your bond. Breaking it could be a fatal mistake. Such a sad way to go. Lie to me even once, and it may be the last thing you ever do.'

Harry shivered, his eyes almost slits as his gut churned and twisted. He knew he had to be convincing. So much rested on his performance. 'I'll always tell you the truth, nothing but the truth, that's a promise from me to you, guaranteed.'

The big man nodded. 'I'm glad to hear it, newbie. Remember those words and never forget them. Etch them on your brain. Engrave them in tablets of stone.'

Harry grimaced, thinking the man insane. Totally insane! Perhaps now was a time for silence. Yes, that seemed best.

'Right, follow me, and do precisely what I tell you to do. You'll stand exactly where I put you, and you'll keep your mouth shut for as long as required. Silence is golden. I don't even want to hear you breathing. You'll stand there, and you'll say nothing, not a single word until you're dismissed back to the dormitory at whatever time the master deems suitable. Everything is within the master's gift. You're his to do with whatever he wishes. Your life is no longer your own. You're here to serve. Is that clear enough for you?'

Harry dry gagged, swallowed, and gagged again. He'd never felt more desperate to get out of there, or so willing to do whatever it took to achieve that aim. 'Yes, yes, you've made yourself perfectly clear. I'm here to serve, I get it. Honestly, I get it. You've said enough.'

'You're my responsibility now, newbie. Everything you do reflects on me as your mentor. My reputation matters to me. It matters a great deal. It's been hard won. Remember that well. Do not even think about letting me down.'

Unquestioning compliance, that's what the bastard wants. Placate the bastard, play the game. 'I won't let you down.'

'Repeat it, and sound as if you mean it this time.'

Harry searched for the right words, any words that helped even in the slightest. He'd never felt less sure of himself. Never so far out of his comfort zone. He knew he had to get out of there, but how? That was the only question that mattered, how? 'I won't let you down. I don't know what else I can say to persuade you of the truth. I'm here for a reason. It's God's will. I'll never let you down.'

Baptist increased the intensity of his grip, digging in his nails, bruising Harry's soft flesh, making him wince as he rushed him towards the waiting gathering with such force that his feet barely touched the ground. 'You'd better not be bullshitting me, newbie. You wouldn't be the first to try. I'm not a trusting man.'

This had to be convincing. 'I wouldn't do that. I'd never do that.'

'For your sake, I hope that's true.'

Harry forced a smile on seeing Achara standing to rigid attention, arms to her side, chest out, chin in the air, behind a line of men to their immediate left. He waved to her with a subtle movement of his hand, but she ignored him, staring into the far-off distance as if she hadn't seen him at all. The girl he'd thought of as an ally seemed strangely oblivious to his existence. As if he didn't matter, as if they'd never met, let alone connected. That bothered Harry. It ate away at him. He felt imaginary icy fingers run up and down his spine, touching his skin and making him shudder. He'd thought Achara offered hope. A potential way out of there. A means of escape. But no, it was all a con, a subterfuge, it seemed she offered nothing at all. It was a new low point. A blow to hope. And just when he'd thought he couldn't feel any worse.

Harry glanced to all sides with furtive darting looks, first one way and then the other, desperately searching for possibilities of freedom, as the big man stood him at the end of the second line of silent men, whispering into his ear at touching distance, skin on skin. Harry could feel Baptist's warm breath on his face as the big man hissed his words, the unmistakable smell of garlic on his breath.

'I know exactly what you're thinking, newbie. I can see inside your head and watch the cogs turning. I can read your thoughts, every predictable idea and notion you entertain is clear to me as if you'd shouted them out loud and proud for everyone to hear. Don't even think about trying to leave this place without the master's prior consent. It would be the worst decision you've ever made.' He raised an arm, pointing to left and right. 'This entire compound is encircled by a high and impenetrable electric fence that's never switched off, not for a single second, day or night. Touch it, and you die, burned to a frazzle. Zap, that's it, you've gone to meet your maker! And there are multiple spotlights that come on and shine bright at the slightest movement in the hours of darkness. They cover all the outside areas of the compound, every inch of it. If you venture outside at any stage, everything you do will be observed right up to the time you earn our trust. The flesh is weak, newbie. The devil will try to influence every decision you make right up to the moment of your enlightenment. Evil is a powerful adversary. We know that full well and act accordingly.'

Harry dropped his head, his body slumping, shoulders over his chest, like a gradually deflating beach toy.

'Chin up, newbie. Come on, it's all for your own good. So, no complaints. You should be grateful to your betters, not indulging in self-pity. The security measures are there to protect the integrity of the community. They keep intruders out, and dissenters in until they know better. Those are good things that you'll come to appreciate and value once you settle in and gain knowledge.'

Harry wanted to run, he was desperate to run, but it was hopeless, absolutely hopeless. He felt sure of it. It stared him in the face. Even if he could escape the big man's clutches, which seemed unlikely, there was nowhere to go. There was just the fence, that deadly fence, and high, impenetrable wooden gates, topped with rolls of blade-sharp razor wire that glinted menacingly in the bright summer sunshine. That wire could slice his flesh to pieces.

Harry just stood there with the others in total silence, physically and emotionally exhausted, head aching, waiting for whatever the day would bring.

He experienced a heady mix of forlorn hope and morale-sapping trepidation that seemed to eat away at him like a thousand rats gnawing at his flesh. Harry knew there was nothing he could do. And so he just stood there, knees knocking and hands shaking despite the warm air, and waited. What other choice was there? What else could he do? He stood and swayed, first one way and then the other, head pounding now, bang, bang, bang, cymbals crashing in his mind, the seconds going on forever as his predicament fully sank in. He pictured a vast and powerful whirlpool, dark water dragging him down, further and further, his life waning as he fought for breath, his arms flailing to no effect. Harry closed his eyes, weeping silent tears as the daydream continued, becoming all too real in his mind. And then a powerful blow to his ribs knocked him sideways and sent him tumbling to the ground, where he lay sobbing until Baptist pulled him to his feet seconds later.

'You need to focus on the now, newbie. Grow a pair of balls. Stop your pathetic snivelling. You're a man, not a baby. A chosen man, with the greatest opportunity of a lifetime stretching out in front of you, if you choose to grasp it.'

'I'm sorry.'

'There's nothing to cry about. You may not know it yet, but you're one of the lucky ones. We all are. We have a future while the rest of the world is doomed to destruction. Now, wipe your face, stand upright, and wait. That's all you have to do.'

Harry looked around him, moving just his eyes. No one else seemed aware of his suffering. They all appeared uninterested. All eyes looked forwards, as if nothing at all had happened, no assault, and no harsh words. As if the big man hadn't done anything at all. They were all standing there in rows for another half an hour or so as the sun shone down and burned their skin. One slightly overweight, middle-aged man with long brown hair parted in the middle, fainted, slumping to the ground as the minutes ticked by. Within seconds two other men rushed towards him, carrying him away into a nearby building, before hurrying back to stand stiffly in line once their function was served. And then, as the gathering continued to wait in hushed expectation, aching, sweating, the anticipation almost perceptible to the touch, the air was suddenly filled with the sound of classical music coming from a tannoy system, drowning out the low diesel throb of a generator meeting the community's electrical needs.

A wave of unbridled excitement passed around the small community of dedicated followers. The classical music continued blaring out for about another ten minutes or so, before suddenly stopping to be replaced moments later by a soaring trumpet fanfare. This was followed by the sound of beating drums, boom, bang, boom, that got louder and louder, reaching a dramatic crescendo as a man Harry thought to be in his mid to late fifties stepped out from a rectangular, single-storey structure between the two dormitory buildings, and walked out to stand in front of the gathering with an unmistakable air of supremacy. As if he knew he was their superior and gloried in the fact.

Harry studied the man's features, taking it all in. He had long grey hair pulled back in a ponytail and a matching salt and pepper beard that reached his chest. His mode of dress was striking and unusual. He wore white just like the others but that's where the comparison ended. His attire was grander. His white robe was edged with gold and purple cloth and reached his ankles. He resembled a Roman emperor at the height of his powers. Harry stared at the robed man, unable to look away as he raised a hand in the air and a pencil-thin girl of about fifteen or sixteen years rushed forwards to stand alongside him, holding a large white sun umbrella above his head. All was silence as the man looked out on the gathered ranks, transferring his gaze from one respectful subject to another as they dropped their heads, focussing on the ground at their feet rather than meet his eyes. And then the man spoke for the first time, as the gathering stood listening, eagerly lapping up his words with an adoration that Harry found impossible to comprehend. Why were they all staring at the robed man with such apparent devotion? As if he were a god in human form. As if he were more than mortal, greater than other men. *Nothing about this place makes sense*, Harry thought. *What the hell is it all about? Are they all mad, brainwashed, deluded? Surely, they must be. None of it makes any sense at all.*

'Good afternoon, my children, it's good to be here with you on this wonderful summer day. All praise to God almighty on high!

We are his chosen people. Never forget that. Never take it for granted. He is looking down on us right now and smiling.'

The entire gathering responded as one, dropping to their knees, fixed expressions of devotion on their adoring faces. 'All praise to the master. We are not worthy. God is great. All praise to the master!'

The robed man smiled, seeming satisfied with the gathering's unified response. 'Thank you, my children. God is watching you from above. He will take note of your obedience and reward you accordingly. Your veneration is to your credit. Now, all stand, that's it, on your feet, up you get. We need to press on.'

All rose as instructed, standing back to rigid attention, as they had before, like a military parade, waiting with bated breath for the master's next pronouncement, as if his words were the most important thing they'd ever heard in their lives. Nothing mattered more.

The robed man smiled contentedly, nodding his approval, waiting for total silence, before continuing in what Harry surmised to be a Yorkshire accent. An accent that seemed to lend an air of normality to an otherwise outlandish situation. 'I have good news to share with you, my children. We have a new member of our exalted community. A young man blessed with youth and vitality that will serve us well as the months pass. Harry, if you could step forward, please. Step forwards and face me. Come on, don't be bashful. Start as you mean to go on. There's no time for dawdling. Let me introduce you to your new family.'

Harry was ushered forwards by Baptist, who led him to within six feet of the master, before forcing him to kneel by pressing down hard on both his shoulders.

The big man hissed into Harry's ear, exuding obvious agitation in tone and demeanour. 'Stay on your knees and look at the ground. Do not under any circumstances look the master in the eye. Have I made myself clear?'

Harry didn't reply at first, but he spoke up quickly when the big man dug his fingers into the soft flesh of his neck, making him wince. 'Yes, sir!'

'Stay there and don't move an inch. Eyes focussed on the ground.'

Harry gulped in the warm air. 'Yes, sir!'

Baptist retreated into the line, standing to attention with the others, as Cameron sauntered forwards, placing an open hand on the top of Harry's bowed head. 'You are blessed, my child. God has spoken to me. You are one of us now. Your new name shall be Shadow. Harry is dead, and a new life is born. You have lived in perpetual darkness for a time. This is your opportunity to emerge into the light. A caterpillar will become a butterfly with God's good grace, a new and beautiful creation.'

Cameron stood Harry up, turning him to face the gathering with a guiding hand. 'The transformation has already begun, my children. Shadow has a new golden glow about him now, as the evil leaves his body to be replaced by light. Look and witness the evidence of God's hand at work! Only the worthy will see, only those with a pure heart. Can you see it, my children? It's happening before your very eyes. Can you see it? Do you have sufficient faith?'

Everyone responded with gleeful rhythmic clapping that gradually increased in volume as chants rang out. 'Yes, yes, yes! Welcome, Shadow, a new life is born. All praise to the master. We are not worthy. God is great! All praise to the master. The master knows all!'

Cameron took a single step back, raising a hand in the air like an assertive police officer stopping traffic. 'Silence! Silence, my children! I have more to share with you on this, God's day.'

Baptist rushed forwards, returning Harry to his original position as two white-clad men in the front row suddenly sprinted away. They came back only seconds later, carrying what looked like a large golden throne that glinted in the sunshine.

Cameron sat himself down, adjusting his position, making himself comfortable. He waved the attendants away once satisfied, as the young girl moved behind the seat, still protecting him from the sun as it shone down, heating her pale skin. Cameron looked out on the gathering with accusing eyes, adopting a well-practised, serious persona that said all they needed to know.

All but Harry knew that look only too well. They understood what it meant, as they stood in trepidation, each fearing the focus of their master's inevitable wrath may fall on them. Each felt his eyes on them as they stood in silent fear. Each thought he was focussed on them and only them, as they searched their troubled minds for any past transgression, however minor, that their master deemed worthy of punishment of one kind or another. It came as a particular relief to all in attendance when Cameron finally spoke again. Each and every one, children included, had discovered over time, that the anticipation of suffering could sometimes seem worse than the pain itself. Their master's utterances were a welcome relief of sorts, however onerous, however terrifying, whatever the possible implications.

Cameron lifted a hand to his ear, cupping it for a few seconds to emphasise the importance of his declaration. 'God has spoken to me, my children. I need you all to listen *very* carefully to what He had to say. The day's pleasantries are over. We have welcomed Shadow to our great community, and now it is time to address more serious matters. Events that have darkened and sullied our small group of disciples. I very much regret to inform you that I have grave news regarding one of our members.'

Cameron waited for his pronouncement to fully sink in for maximum impact before finally continuing, revelling in the gathering's obvious discomfort as each member trembled with the fear of it all.

Cameron suddenly reached out, pointing with a jabbing digit at a slight, pale, yellow-haired young man standing to attention in the front row. 'I very much regret to inform you that River has failed to live up to the high standards expected of our community. I have no option but to tell you that he has let himself down. He has let all of you down. He has let me down. And worst of all, yes, worst of all, he has let God down! Did you hear what I said, my children? River has failed us in the worst possible way!'

A loud murmur of disapproval filled the air as the gathering waited for their master to continue, as he inevitably would.

'God has told me that in the early hours of the morning River attempted to leave the compound without my prior consent. He broke the rules, my children. He cheated us all! Is there a worse crime? He knew the conditions of membership, he knew of the high standards we expect of our group, and yet he attempted to leave us with no consideration for the needs and well-being of the community that has given him so very much. River is possessed by a devil, an evil spirit, a demon, a spectre from the darkest corner of hell. What other explanation is there, my children? River's dark thoughts allowed the evil in. No, no, he invited the evil in! Did you hear me, my children? Has the enormity of his failings fully sunk in? River's dishonesty and subterfuge rendered him vulnerable to the dark forces that inhabit this world. It is his responsibility. His, and his alone!'

The jeers got louder and louder, filling the entire compound with vibrating sound until the master raised a hand to silence them.

'River's thoughtless actions have brought evil into our midst. His disloyal behaviour has unleashed ungodly forces where there was only light and love. And that, my children, is worthy of punishment. God has taught me that some things cannot be forgiven or forgotten. This is one of those times. River's failings are far too serious for that.'

Loud chants rang out now, as every eye focussed on the ashen-faced young man, who sank to his knees, shaking his head as if in denial. He was begging for forgiveness, pleading for mercy more in hope than expectation. But nobody heard.

The chants got louder. 'River has failed us! River has failed us! River has failed us!'

Cameron looked out on his congregation, boosted by his manipulative prowess, wallowing in the young man's obvious distress, shouting out his words above the din. 'Should we punish River for his failings? What do you say, my children? Should we drive the sin from his mind and body? Should we beat it out of him until the dark and malevolent spirit possessing him leaves us, to return to the nether world from which it came?'

The young man collapsed to the ground, knees clutched tightly to his chest as a chorus of hisses and boos were followed by the sound of further rhythmic chanting, the implications of which were all too familiar. 'Drive it out! Drive it out! Drive the evil out!'

Urine pooled under River, staining his white cotton trousers as the chants got louder, finally reaching a crashing crescendo as the gathered throng formed a tight circle around him, screaming, 'Unworthy! Unworthy! Unworthy! Drive it out! Drive it out! Drive the demon out!'

Harry stood and watched in growing horror and disbelief as the gathered members of the community moved slowly forward. They closed in one step at a time, a powerful wave of hot and angry bodies, kicking, punching, gouging, scratching, stamping and biting, as their young victim huddled helplessly on the hard ground, blood pouring from his various wounds as the assault continued with ever increasing ferocity. Harry was unable to look away as the attack continued for a full minute that seemed to go on forever. Harry stumbled backwards, clutching his gut, retching, throwing up again and again until there was nothing left but bile. He looked at the electric fence and then at the high gates with their razor wire on top, considering escape like never before, while the attention of the others was focussed on River. But Baptist was watching him and only him. The big man was standing with his back to the crowd, staring at Harry with the unmistakable hint of a smile playing on his lips. As if nothing of significance had happened. As if the young man wasn't lying, beaten, battered and blood-soaked on the unforgiving concrete parade ground just feet away from where they both stood. Harry was reminded of stories of Roman excesses as the unwelcome scene continued to unfold in front of him. He was contemplating the madness of it all, the horror of it all, his revulsion, his feelings of panic, the merciless nature of the brutal mass assault, when Cameron rose slowly to his feet, raising a hand in the air for the third time.

'Stop! That's sufficient! God is satisfied. The devil is beaten, defeated by the blows of the righteous. Our brother has suffered enough, my children. His punishment will suffice. Return to your lines. Come on now, back you all go! River has paid the appropriate price for his transgression. And he will learn a valuable lesson from the experience. Evil is defeated. The devil has slithered back from whence he came. River will be placed in the hole and allowed to atone through self-reflection and prayer. Now is the time for mercy.'

The gathered crowd responded quickly to their master's command. They returned immediately to their original positions, sweating, panting hard and blood-spattered. They stood back to stiff attention as River, or David as he'd previously been known to friends and family, lay groaning incoherently on the red-stained concrete, lost to the welcome annihilation of oblivion. Dark blood flowed freely from the young man's nose, mouth, ears and scalp, his features strangely distorted, his face a swollen pulp, unrecognisable as the carefree, good-looking young science graduate who'd arrived at the community compound only months before.

Harry stood there and stared, not quite able to believe what he'd witnessed, as the victim lay just feet away in a bloody, groaning heap, clinging onto life as it threatened to drain away. Harry desperately wanted to approach the unfortunate victim, to whisper words of soothing comfort into his ear, to provide what help he could. But he couldn't move. He felt welded to the spot, frozen, incapacitated by the fear and shock of it all. He was still standing there, staring at the bruised and battered victim with haunted, glazed eyes, when Baptist hurried towards him, dragging him back into line and standing next to him at touching distance.

Cameron strode first one way and then the other, to the left, to the right, and back again, stopping at various intervals to study one member of the community or another, the umbrella still held high above his head by the attendant girl, who hurried after him with nervous, faltering steps.

Every member of the group dropped their heads, lowering their eyes with the utmost urgency as their master approached them with a blank expression on his very ordinary face. He continued his inspection for another ten minutes or so before finally returning to his gold-painted wooden seat. He spoke again, clearly articulating each word with evident enthusiasm. 'Thank you, my children. The punishment of transgressors is a regrettable but necessary process that benefits us all. The devil came into our midst and was driven out by the blessed servants of God.'

The air was filled with the sound of rousing cheers that echoed around the compound.

'Enough! Silence! We are almost done for today, but not quite. River will now spend fourteen days in the ground, devoid of light and fed only limited sustenance. Then he will be allowed back into the community. If he is truly repentant, that should provide more than sufficient time for his body to heal, and for the appropriate degree of self-reflection on his part. He has failed dismally and needs to look inside himself with a critical eye. He needs to beg for God's forgiveness. And he needs to beg for *our* forgiveness too. This is his final opportunity to attain the necessary standards expected of us all. His last chance of redemption. There are limits to my capacity for forgiveness and to God's good grace. Now take him away, you know the routine, get him out of my sight, put him in the hole and secure the hatch. I have looked at him for long enough.'

River was carried away by the same two men who'd transported the wooden throne earlier in the proceedings. It was something they'd done before. Something with which they were entirely familiar. They did it in silence and with practised efficiency, leaving dark red stains on the concrete where River had lain.

'Thank you, my children, you've done well in extremely challenging circumstances. Punishing a brother or sister is not easy, but it is necessary. Your obedience is to your credit. Now return to your allocated tasks. You are here to serve and grow. Never forget. Never lose focus. You have jobs to do. It's time to get on with them. Work purifies the soul.'

Everyone backed slowly away, heads bowed, staring at the ground, as their master strolled back towards the building from which he'd first appeared, the white umbrella still shading him from a bright sun shining down from a blue and cloudless sky. The young girl, only three months past her fifteenth birthday, lowered the umbrella on entering a spacious hallway, holding it tightly with a hand that wouldn't stop shaking. She hesitated, keen to leave at the earliest opportunity, but not wanting to irritate her master even slightly. 'Shall I leave you now, master? I haven't finished cutting the grass on the north bank. I need to finish before the light fades.'

Cameron strode into a comfortably furnished lounge area, speaking without looking back, as she stood and waited, fidgeting with her cuff, staring at the wall.

'No, I don't think so, my child. Shower, apply some perfume, wrap a clean towel around yourself, and join me in the bedroom. I have stiffness in my back and my muscles ache. You can provide a therapeutic massage. Nice and firmly, mind, just like your mother. It's something she's good at. Something in which she excels. Her entire body becomes a healing tool with God's help. I doubt you possess the same therapeutic skills, not yet, not with such limited experience. But not to worry. I'm prepared to tolerate your inevitable fumbling. You'll learn and improve as time goes by. I'll look forward to that.'

The young girl felt her heart thumping in her throat, a sinking feeling deep in the pit of her stomach as she retreated towards the door, the umbrella still in hand. 'But the grass, master, it won't stop growing. I need to cut it. What about the grass?'

Cameron turned to look at her with a dismissive sneer that made her shudder. 'You're here to serve. Never forget that. It's God's will. You saw what happened to River. You understand the potential consequences of disobedience. It would not be a good idea to disappoint me again. Now, do exactly as you're told. There's a good girl. That's all you've got to do.'

10

Harry's mother knocked on the front door of his student digs for almost five minutes without receiving an answer. She knocked again, harder this time, pounding the door with the side of one fist, hoping to be heard above the rock music she didn't recognise or appreciate coming from inside. Sally Gilmore bent easily at the waist and peered through the letterbox for a second time, yelling out at the top of her voice, high-pitched, almost screeching, increasingly desperate to be heard above the din.

She'd practically given up on receiving a response when a first-floor window suddenly opened, and a young man of about Harry's age, with curly black hair that perfectly framed his impish face, looked down, squinting as the summer sun made him blink.

'Yeah, I'm up here. Where's the fire?'

Sally called out, struggling to be heard above the noise. 'I'm, err, I'm Mrs Gilmore, Harry's mother. I've been trying to get hold of him. Any idea where he is?'

The student's brow furrowed as he leaned out a little further. 'What?'

'I'm Harry's mum, Harry's mum!'

He shook his head. 'No, sorry, I can't hear a word you're saying.'

She clamped her hands over her ears in exasperation. 'The music, turn off the music!'

A look of recognition suddenly dawned on his youthful face. 'Ah, yeah, the music. Give me a second, I'll switch it off.'

Sally Gilmore stood and waited, curling her toes, and then tapping her foot on the pavement until he reappeared a short time later.

'Sorry about that, force of habit. I'm a massive metal fan. What can I do for you?'

Sally blew the air from her mouth with a loud whistle. She spoke more calmly now, her chest rising and falling in rhythmic motion as she attempted to control her mounting anxiety. 'I said, I'm Harry's mum. He's not answering his phone. I've been trying to get hold of him for almost a week.'

'Yeah, I haven't seen him either. I can't help you, sorry.'

Sally felt like screaming when the student closed the window and disappeared from sight. She heard the music ring out as before, but somewhat quieter this time. She banged the door again with all the force she could muster, pounding it with a newfound strength until it vibrated in its frame. She kept hitting it with increasing frustration until it was opened by the same young man, who stood facing her with a look of puzzlement on his face.

'Look, I'm sorry I can't help you. I don't know what more I can tell you.'

'But you are Harry's friend, yes?'

He nodded. 'Well, yeah.'

'When did you last see him?'

'About, err, ten o'clock last Friday morning.'

'How did he seem?'

'Does it matter?'

Her expression hardened. 'Yes, I think it very probably does.'

He allowed the doorframe to support his weight. 'He seemed a bit wracked off about something or other. I don't know what exactly.'

'You've got no idea, none at all?'

'No, not a clue, I did ask what was up, but he didn't want to talk about it. He's like that sometimes. Keeps stuff to himself. But then I guess you already know that.'

'Surely he must have said something to you.'

'Just that he was heading into town.'

She raised a hand to her chin. 'And that's the last time you saw or heard from him?'

'Yeah, I thought it was odd he'd left all his stuff and didn't say bye, but I assumed he'd gone back home for a bit. There's nothing more I can tell you.'

He went to close the door, but she stepped forward, placing one foot in the hallway. 'Can I come in and have a look around Harry's room?'

'Oh, I don't know about that.'

Sally lowered her head, and for a moment, he thought she may start weeping. 'Please, there may be clues as to where he's gone. I don't know what else I can do.'

He thought for a moment. 'Do you really think it's necessary?'

She nodded frantically. 'Yes, yes, I do. Disappearing for days on end isn't like him. He usually keeps in touch. He rings or texts most days. I'm trying to stay positive, but I'm beginning to think something may have gone horribly wrong.'

'Oh, come on. You're probably worrying about nothing.'

Sally closed her eyes for a beat. 'Can I just come in and have a look around, please? I really think it may help. I'm worried sick.'

The young student stood aside to allow her to pass, waving her in. 'He could have lost his phone, I suppose. I lost mine a few days back before finding it again.'

'Do you think he has?'

'I don't know, I'm just thinking out loud. But you've got to admit it's a possibility. He's always losing stuff. Especially when he's pissed.'

She turned to face him, looking older. 'Has he started drinking again?'

'Oh shit, maybe I shouldn't have said anything. He did say something about not drinking alcohol.' He laughed. 'I thought he may be avoiding buying another round at the time.'

Sally rushed towards the staircase, looking back before ascending. 'Which room is his?'

'Up the stairs, second door on the left. You can't miss it.'

'Thank you. I really appreciate your help. It means a lot.'

'Fancy a coffee? I'm making one, anyway.'

She smiled thinly on reaching the small landing, looking back, experiencing a flashback to her own student days, which now seemed so very long ago. Before life happened. Before time blunted her edges. 'Thank you, it's appreciated. I'll have a cup of tea if there's one on offer.'

'Milk and sugar?'

'Just a splash of milk, please.'

He grinned, glad she'd changed the mood. 'It'll be waiting for you in the kitchen whenever you're ready.'

Sally approached Harry's bedroom door with a look of anticipation on her face. She didn't know what she expected to find, but she thought she'd find something. It was an instinct of sorts, no more than that. Deep in her psyche she knew she'd discover something informative, something notable which would help tell a story. Sally held one hand to her abdomen as she turned the handle and pushed the door open. She entered Harry's bedroom with a growing sense of foreboding that made no sense to her at all. It was just an ordinary room. A room so very typical of a male student's abode, with its posters of beautiful, scantily clad women in seductive poses covering two of the four walls. She shook her head, resigned to what she saw as the inevitable obsessions of youth, and sighed as she turned in a tight circle.

Sally took it all in for the first time. The untidy bed, the piles of dirty washing in one corner, the soiled mugs on his desk, and a frayed carpet littered with books and pieces of paper. It was badly in need of hoovering. It wasn't exactly what she'd hoped for, but it didn't surprise her a great deal. She pondered that girls still matured so much more quickly than boys despite all of society's changes. Harry was still a teenager, after all. It seemed he'd reverted to type as soon as he'd left the family home. Or maybe the posters were a deception of sorts. A show put on for his new mates. An effort to fit in, to be one of the lads. Maybe Simone wasn't such a significant influence after all.

Sally looked in the sideboard drawers first, sorting through various items. There were condoms, pens, a course timetable, a few copper coins, but not much more. Certainly nothing that would alleviate her angst to any degree. She moved on to the Victorian wardrobe, finding nothing but clothes, and then dropped to her knees, peering under the bed, but there was nothing significant to see there either, just a few cobwebs and dust that made her sneeze. Sally searched the entire room again for a second time, but with the same negative results.

She sat on the edge of the unmade bed for a few seconds, gathering her thoughts. Surely there must be something, a clue somewhere. What was she missing? She approached the room's only window and looked out, hoping to see her much-loved son strolling down the street towards the house without a care in the world. But of course, he wasn't there. Sally didn't see anyone at all. It was time to go back downstairs. Time to drink her tea. Time to ask the right questions. The questions that may help her find her son.

Sally was about to leave the room when something unquantifiable told her to check the floor for one final time. She almost ignored her inclination, thinking it false hope born of desperation. But she changed her mind at the last second. *Why not look again?* There was little, if anything, to lose. Just a few seconds of her time. And the feeling was so strong, so insistent. Maybe it shouldn't be ignored.

Sally took her bifocal spectacles from her handbag, perching them on the tip of her nose. When she looked around her, she spotted the brown plastic medicine bottle almost immediately, admonishing herself for not putting on her glasses before now. There it was lying on the multicoloured carpet close to Harry's single bed. It was calling out to her as if highlighted by a spotlight. Sally reached down and picked the bottle up, holding it out in front of her and asking herself how she could ever have missed it in the first place. And the bottle was half full. *Oh shit.* It must be his current prescription. Surely he wouldn't have stopped taking the tablets by choice. Not after all this time. No, no, of course he wouldn't. He relied on the damned things. They were his crutch in life. He'd need them, wherever he was, whatever he was doing. *Please be safe, Harry, please be safe. This isn't good. It isn't good at all.*

The young student handed Sally a chipped mug of freshly brewed tea with a nervous grin. 'Did you have any luck?'

She sat at the breakfast bar, balanced on a high stool, holding the medicine bottle up in plain sight, with a single tear rolling down her face. 'Did Harry mention he takes medication?'

'Yeah, he did say something. But he didn't say what it was for and I didn't ask. I'm sure he'd have told me if he wanted to.'

She shook the bottle. 'It's something he needs to take every day without fail. He's going to be in danger without them. I'm even more worried now than I was when I first arrived.'

'Oh, really? I had no idea they were that important.'

Sally dropped the bottle into her handbag, asking herself if she'd said too much. She felt conflicted. The last thing she wanted to do was betray her son's confidence. Some things were best kept secret. It seemed he valued his privacy. 'Look, this is getting serious. I can't stress that enough. I really need to find him. If you know of anything that happened, anything at all, now's the time to tell me.'

'Try not to worry about it, he'll turn up, it's just a matter of time.'

She sipped her tea, wetting her mouth, frustrated by his apparent lack of urgency. 'Do you think something was worrying him? Something I may not know about? If he's in trouble, he'd want me to know about it. You can tell me anything, however embarrassing. I was young myself once. Please don't hold anything back.'

The student pressed his lips together, giving it genuine consideration, shaking his head. 'No, not that I can think of, no big deal. He wasn't too confident about passing his exams. But then we all feel like that to some extent. It's not like he was crapping himself or anything. He always gets decent marks in his essays without too much trouble. I think he's the brightest of all of us. He always does okay. I'm sure the exams won't be any different.'

Sally nodded. 'Yes, he's a bright lad when he applies himself. His A-level results were better than I'd dared to hope – three As. I was so proud of him. I think they'd have been A stars if he'd worked a little harder.'

He tilted his head back, draining half his mug and laughing. 'He kept that one quiet. I didn't realise we had a genius in the house.'

Sally clutched his arm momentarily, changing the mood,

willing him to help her. 'Can you think of anywhere he may have gone? What about somewhere with Simone? I've been trying to get hold of her, but she's not replying either. I know she's received my messages, but she doesn't get back to me whatever I say. Do you think they may have gone off somewhere together? I feel ridiculous even asking this, but is there something they're doing that they don't want me to know about? I'm ready to believe almost anything at this point.'

He jerked his head back. 'They've split up. Haven't you heard?'

Sally's mouth fell open. 'What? Harry didn't say anything, not a word. I thought they were in it for the long haul. Do you know what went wrong?'

'Well, he said the breakup was mutual, but I'm not so sure. I think she may have dumped him, to be honest. I saw her out with another bloke a couple of nights back, a right flash git in a business suit. He looked at least twenty years older than her. I don't think he was short of a few quid if you know what I'm saying. You know, the sugar daddy type, flashing the cash. They were all over each other.' He laughed humourlessly. 'It made me want to puke. It was only a couple of weeks ago she was telling Harry how much she loved him. What's that about?'

'Did she say anything to you?'

He shook his head. 'No, I can't stand the snooty cow. She thinks she's too good for the likes of me. You know, people who weren't born with a silver spoon in their mouths. We didn't speak, which suited me just fine. I'd be quite happy if I never saw her again.'

Sally shifted on her stool, crossing and uncrossing her legs, unable to get comfortable. 'I only met her the once, but she seemed all right to me.'

'She must have been putting on an act. If she'd been herself, you wouldn't have liked her.'

'I didn't realise she was like that.'

'Oh, yeah, big time, she has been from the first day I met her. She thinks she's something special, that one. She likes to impress. And it's always with an end goal in mind.'

Sally sipped her tea, still struggling to digest the revelation. 'Did Harry seem upset by the split?'

'Not that he told me about. There's no shortage of girls in our year. He'll meet someone new soon enough. He should have given Simone the push long ago in my opinion. He couldn't do any worse.'

Sally looked into the far-off distance, deep in contemplative thought. 'Are you certain there's nothing you can think of that could help me find him, nothing at all? Think hard please. This really matters to me. I'm starting to get seriously worried.'

He shook his head, draining his mug before placing it on the countertop and standing. 'No, I don't think so, there's nothing, sorry. I've told you everything I know. If anything comes up, I'll get in touch. And I'll talk to Simone when I get the chance. I'll tell her to contact you as a matter of urgency. Hopefully, she'll respond.'

'Thank you, that's very good of you.'

'You're welcome. It's the least I can do.'

Sally took her recently upgraded mobile from her handbag, giving him her number and recording his for future reference, just in case she needed it. 'You haven't told me your name.'

'It's Luke, Luke Irvine.'

She nodded her recognition. 'Ah, yes, okay, Harry's mentioned you.'

'We've been housemates since the first day of the course.'

'You'll let me know if you hear anything, yes? You'll do that for me, won't you, Luke?'

The student walked back in the direction of the front door. 'Yeah, no problem, I'll ask around. He's bound to turn up. When I hear something, I'll message you straight away. You'll be the first to know.'

Sally hesitated, stalling as she stepped out into the street. 'Do you promise? Will you give me your word?'

He reached out and shook her hand, holding it right up to the time it was no longer comfortable. 'If it makes you feel better, then yes, I promise. I'll put the word out. And if and when I hear of Harry's whereabouts, I'll tell you. I give you my word, guaranteed.'

'I'm thinking of going to the police.'

'Really?'

She hurried towards her car parked in a nearby side street, thinking out loud, her words lost on the breeze as he closed the door. 'Oh yes, I don't know what else I can do. It really couldn't be more urgent. It's their job to find him. If not the police, then who?'

11

Detective Inspector Laura Kesey unwrapped a third chocolate truffle and placed it in her mouth, resisting the impulse to chew as her phone rang out and broke her concentration. She lifted the receiver to her face and spoke with a nasal, Brummie accent that some Welsh colleagues still found difficult to decipher despite its growing familiarity. 'CID, how can I help you?'

'Hello, ma'am, it's Sandra at the front desk.'

'For goodness sake, Sandra, I've told you to call me Laura. How many times have I got to say it? Ma'am makes me feel about a hundred years old.'

'Yes, ma'am.'

Kesey shook her head, manoeuvring the melting chocolate to one side of her mouth with her tongue, savouring the creamy sweetness. 'What can I do for you, Sandra? You only just caught me in.'

'Oh, are you going anywhere nice?'

Kesey laughed. 'Oh, I wish, just a meeting.'

The receptionist blew her nose loudly before responding. 'Sorry, Laura, my allergies are playing up again. It's the time of year for it. Give me a second.' She sneezed, once, then again. 'There, that's better... right, I've got a Mrs Sally Gilmore here with me, who says that her son's missing.'

The detective stiffened, glancing at the silver-framed colour photo of her own two-year-old son on her cluttered desk, feeling genuine empathy for the mother. A missing child must be the worst feeling in the world. 'Okay, you've got my attention. How old is he?'

She heard Sandra say, 'How old's your son, Mrs Gilmore?'

The distraught mother provided the answer, adding additional information she thought relevant.

Sandra returned her attention to her call. 'He's nineteen, Laura. Harry Gilmore, he's a student at the university studying for a sociology degree.'

Kesey relaxed back in her seat, running a hand through her short brown hair. 'Oh, come on, Sandra, he's nineteen, not nine. Ask one of the uniformed officers to have a word with her. There must be someone about. It's not a CID matter. I don't need to get involved unless there's more to it.'

'The mother asked for you by name. She said she teaches you yoga every Tuesday evening at the library. You're one of her best students, quite the star pupil, apparently.'

'Ah, yeah, of course, Sally Gilmore. I know who you're talking about now. I only think of her by her first name.'

Sandra coughed, clearing her throat. 'So, what do you want me to tell her?'

Kesey pushed up the sleeve of her navy-blue jumper, checking the stainless steel Swiss sports watch received from Janet, her partner of five years, the previous Christmas. 'Oh, I guess I'd better pop down and see her myself. Are any of the interview rooms free?'

Sandra checked the book. 'Rooms one and three.'

'Right, put her in room one and tell her I'll be with her in five minutes. I need to give social services a ring and tell them I'm going to be late.'

'I can do that for you if you like. I've got the number here somewhere.'

'No, you're all right, thanks, Sandra. I need to have a quick word with the team manager. There's a child protection case I'm not too happy with.'

Sandra nodded in reflexive response before putting the phone down. She still hadn't got used to the boss's new way of doing things. It wasn't so very long ago she'd insisted on the use of her title. Oh, well, such was life. It seemed she'd relaxed into the role.

Sandra rose from her seat and smiled, keen to put Sally at ease, or as near as possible given the circumstances. 'Come with me, Mrs Gilmore, DI Kesey won't be too long; you can tell me all about the yoga classes.' She patted her tummy. 'I've been thinking about losing a bit of weight for the summer. Do you fancy a cup of tea while you're waiting?'

Sally wiped a tear from her cheek. 'That would be lovely. Thank you for being so kind.'

Sandra held open the interview room door. 'Take a seat, and I'll make that tea. Milk and sugar?'

'Just milk, please.'

'Okey-dokey, I'll be back with you before you know it.'

Kesey entered interview room one to be met by a tearful, middle-aged woman with shoulder-length dyed blonde hair, who rose to her feet with a forced, swiftly disappearing smile that looked far from convincing. Sally met Kesey's eyes with a haunted look, the words pouring from her mouth at breakneck speed, like a torrent she couldn't hope to slow even if she tried. 'Hello, Laura, I never thought I'd see you like this. Not at work, not at the police station. I really hope you can help me. I've never been so worried in my life. It's good of you to see me so very quickly. I know how busy you must be.'

Kesey placed a supportive hand on each of Sally's shoulders. 'Not at all, it's the least I can do. Now take a seat and tell me what this is all about.'

Sally sat as instructed, dabbing at each of her eyes in turn with a paper hankie taken from her handbag, smearing black mascara across one cheek. 'It's Harry, my son, I haven't been able to get hold of him for over a week. It's really starting to bother me. I don't know what to do for the best.'

Kesey poised a rollerball pen above her police-issue pocketbook.' He's nineteen, yes? An adult in law. Why so worried? I know what I was like at that age. My parents sometimes didn't hear from me for weeks.'

Sally screwed up her face. 'I really don't know where to start.'

Kesey smiled thinly. 'How about at the beginning? I usually find that's best. Just spell out your concerns, and we'll progress matters from there.'

'I last spoke to Harry at about half past seven last Wednesday evening. I can remember the time because the phone rang just as *Coronation Street* was due to start. I've tried contacting his mobile numerous times since then, but without success. I'm beginning to wish I'd come to talk to you before now. I'll never forgive myself if he's come to any harm. I don't know what I'd do without him.'

Kesey tapped the tip of her biro on the table, considering her choice of words. 'It's only a few days, and he's a nineteen-year-old lad. He's probably off somewhere having a good time if he's like any of the students I knew at college.'

'I really don't think so.'

'Okay, I'm listening.'

Sally sipped her tea. 'Harry usually contacts me almost every day in one way or another. You know, either by calling at the house to say hello, speaking by phone, or texting. There's only him and me since my husband died, and we're close, we always have been. He's not your typical nineteen-year-old. I need you to understand that. It's just not like him not to stay in touch, and his phone's dead. It has been for days. He's usually welded to the thing. He hardly goes five minutes without looking at it. Something's wrong, I know it is. It's the only explanation that makes any sense at all.'

Kesey brushed non-existent fluff from her skirt. 'And you're saying you last spoke to him on that Wednesday evening, correct?'

'Yes, and he really seemed his old self. I'm sure I'd have known if there was anything seriously wrong. I'd have heard it in his voice. I really wish I'd asked. I wish I'd paid him more attention when I had the chance. To be honest, I was in a hurry to get back to the television. I feel terrible about that now. What sort of mother does that make me? I wish I could turn the clock back. I'd do things very differently if I could.'

Kesey reached across the table and patted her hand. 'Everything's clearer when we look back on it. You couldn't possibly have known what was going to happen. Let's concentrate on trying to find him. There's no point in beating yourself up. What's that going to achieve?'

Sally nodded. 'Yes, I understand what you're saying. I know there's a logic to it. And I have tried to find him. I should probably tell you that Harry's housemate saw him on the Friday morning, two days after I'd spoken to him. I've just come from there now. His name's Luke, Luke Irvine. He told me Harry said he was going into Carmarthen. But he hasn't seen or heard from him since.'

Kesey opened her pocketbook at the first blank page. 'Okay, let's try to make sense of what's happened. It's never a good idea to rule anything out without good reason. Do you know of anything that was worrying your son? Anything at all?'

Sally sighed. 'He's never been the most together boy in the

world, not since the death of his dad. They were close. The loss hit Harry hard. I don't think he's ever really gotten over it, not completely. There's a sadness about him these days, as if there's a dark cloud hanging over him, even when he smiles. He hides it well most of the time, but it's there.'

'And you think that may be significant?'

Sally took her son's brown plastic medicine bottle from her handbag and placed it on the table. 'There's no point in pretending that everything's sweetness and light. Harry has a history of depression. It's been devastating at times, although the pills have helped.' She held up the bottle. 'I found these on his bedroom floor at his digs. And that's a problem. I really don't know how he's going to cope without them.'

Kesey looked across the table with genuine sympathy. 'You don't think he could have another bottle?'

Sally shook her head. 'I can't see how he could. I pick up his prescriptions for him to save him bother and reassure myself that he doesn't run out.'

'Okay, I get why you're concerned. Is there anything else you can tell me? Even if it seems unimportant. Tell me everything you can think of and let me decide if it matters. I find it usually works better that way. Even the most insignificant of details can sometimes prove to be crucial to an investigation.'

Sally tensed. 'Investigation? Oh, God, you're as concerned as I am. This is all starting to seem horribly serious. I shouldn't have left things as long as I did.'

Kesey was quick to respond. 'Sorry, investigation's a technical term, that's all, a force of habit. What I meant to say, is that we're going to look for Harry. We're going to do everything we can to find him as soon as practicably possible. And you can help us do that by answering my questions with as much clarity as you possibly can. Are you ready to move on?'

'Yes, absolutely! What do you need to know?'

'Do you know of anything else that could be bothering him, anything at all?'

'Um, yes, Harry's split up with his girlfriend. I only found that out today. Luke mentioned it. And he's a bit worried about his exam results, but then that's nothing new. He's always been a bit of a worrier. But he's a bright boy. A psychologist ran some tests a few years back. Harry's got an IQ in the top two per cent of the population, although he never really makes the most of the intelligence he was given. He cruises through the course because he can. I'm certain he knows he's going to pass deep down.'

Kesey picked up the pill bottle, holding it close to her eyes, reading the label. 'How long has he been taking these for?'

'Um, it's, err, it's been several years now.'

'And that's since the death of his father, yes?'

'Yes, that's right... sorry, I thought I'd already made that clear.'

'How old was he?'

'Harry or his father?'

Kesey stifled a yawn, interrupted sleep taking its toll. 'Both, if you don't mind me asking?'

'Harry was twelve and Jack forty-one. My husband was one of life's good guys. He always put his family first. Life can be so very unfair sometimes. We met when we were teenagers. I still miss him terribly.'

Kesey rested her elbows on the table. 'What happened, how did he die?'

Sally's face paled as the memories flooded back. 'Jack was involved in a car crash. Head on with a lorry on an icy road. His spleen ruptured. He never stood a chance. The poor man was dead on arrival at the hospital. I never even had the opportunity to say goodbye. That's one of my biggest regrets.'

The detective looked at her with concern. 'I'm sorry for your loss.'

'Thank you.'

'Okay, let's get on... have you contacted the university authorities?'

'Yes, I rang from the car before coming in. I was able to speak to one of Harry's lecturers, a Dr Russel Richards, who's head of his course. He said there'd be no reason for any of the tutors to have any contact with Harry until the start of the new term, unless Harry initiated it himself. That makes sense if you think about it. Harry's exam results will be e-mailed to him by one of the administrative staff. Dr Russel said that he wanted to help but couldn't. And I really think he's right. What on earth could he do?'

'Did the doctor seem concerned at all? Was he aware of any problems you haven't told me about?'

'No, nothing at all, not in the slightest, or at least nothing he shared with me. I did ask, and he said Harry seemed to have settled in very well. He was expecting great things.'

Kesey nodded. 'I may have a word with Russel myself at some point if I think it's necessary.'

'I don't know what else he could tell you. Surely he'd have told me if he'd known anything. Why wouldn't he?'

'What about Harry's university friends? Is there anyone you think I should speak to, other than this Irvine character?'

'Well, there's Simone, of course, Harry's ex. She doesn't seem to want to talk to me at all. Believe me, I've tried. Perhaps you'd have more luck than I've had.'

'Have you got her contact details?'

Sally took her phone from her bag, providing Simone's number as requested.

'You haven't got an address?'

'No, sorry, I know she lives here in town somewhere, but I've got no idea where.'

'Look, I've got to ask... has Harry ever had thoughts of suicide?'

Sally closed her eyes for a beat before replying. 'He self-harmed for a time when he was twelve and thirteen. He used to cut his arms with anything sharp he could get hold of. He said it made him feel better in some strange way he couldn't explain. A psychologist at the child guidance clinic told me it's a way of translating emotional pain into physical pain. Rather than feel too much or too little, it can help people feel as if they exist again. It seems it's one thing they can control in a random world. It didn't make a lot of sense to me at the time. But I think it does now when I look back on it. It's sad, really. It's a far more common problem than most people realise.'

Kesey noted the mother's response with a rapid movement of her pen. 'Did the psychologist prescribe the medication?'

'Can they do that?'

'Um, I'm not sure, to be honest. Was it someone else?'

Sally nodded. 'Yes, the tablets came later. The psychologist really seemed to have helped for a time, but Harry deteriorated again shortly after his fourteenth birthday. He developed an all-consuming fear of death that became an obsession. He started talking to his dead father on a regular basis. You know, actual conversations as if Jack was there in the room. It really shook me up for a time. Actually, that's an understatement, it freaked me out. I didn't know what to do or say for the best. Harry just wasn't the boy I'd known. One tragic event blew our lives apart.'

'That sounds tough.'

'Oh, it was. The toughest time of my life.'

'And that led to the tablets?'

Sally raised a hand to her throat as the past closed in and surrounded her mercilessly. 'Yes, Harry was prescribed the antidepressants by his GP while awaiting another appointment at the clinic. She'd been our doctor for years. I think she felt almost as worried as I did.'

'And he's still taking them after all this time?'

'Yes, it's been five long years. I don't think it was ever meant to work out that way. But Harry quickly became reliant on them, that's the truth of it. He's tried to come off them a couple of times, but without success. He's fragile, I think that's the best way of explaining it. He puts on a brave face, he seems like one of the lads, but it doesn't take very much to knock him down again.'

Kesey's concerns were increasing with every new fact Sally shared. If she found the boy alive, it would be a miracle. She had to ask. There was no way of sugar-coating this particular pill. 'Has Harry ever actually attempted suicide?'

Sally shook her head. 'No, no, he hasn't. He's talked about it, he's threatened it, he even put it in a letter once, but that's as far as it's ever gone. I guess I've got to be grateful for that.'

'When was the last time he threatened to kill himself?'

Sally raised her eyes to the ceiling. 'Oh, it's been, what, just over three years. It was on the anniversary of his father's funeral. We'd visited the grave together to lay flowers. I thought the worst times were behind us, I really did. How wrong can you be?' She began weeping. 'Oh, God, you don't think he's dead, do you?'

Kesey knew she couldn't make promises she wasn't in a position to keep. She'd once done that as an inexperienced officer, and it had cost her. It was a hard lesson she wouldn't ever forget. 'I'm going to do all I can to find your son, starting today.'

Sally spoke through her tears. 'So, what happens now?'

'Let's start with a description, the more detailed, the better. I'll get it circulated on a countrywide basis as a matter of priority.'

'Thank you, Laura. Thank you so very much.'

'You're welcome... now, let's make a start.'

Sally picked up her phone. She tapped a finger on the photo app, searching for a suitable image that clearly showed her son's face. Once satisfied, she pushed the mobile across the table. 'That was taken about a year ago, just before he started university.'

Kesey studied the picture and then sent it to her official force email address. Harry was smiling in the image. But there was an unmistakable sadness about him that touched Kesey's heart. 'He's a good-looking lad.'

'Yes, he is, he's following his father. He looked much the same at that age.'

'The photo's going to help us. Now, just a few more details and I'll get the description circulated.'

'What do you need?'

'How tall is he?'

'Five foot, eleven inches.'

'And his weight?'

'Harry has never eaten enough for my liking. And I think it's been even worse since he's been living in digs. He's only about ten stone at most. He's never had much of an appetite. Not even as a child before, well, you know, before the accident.'

Kesey raised an eyebrow. 'We're probably not going to need this, but I have to ask, it's a matter of procedure.'

Sally guessed what was coming next. 'Just say what you need to say, Laura. Nothing you can say is going to make me feel any worse than I already do. Anything that helps.'

'Has Harry got any distinguishing marks?'

Sally took a long, slow breath, her chest tightening. 'Just the scars on his arms that I mentioned. They've healed well and faded. The GP recommended a massage oil that Harry rubbed in every night before bed. They're only noticeable if you look for them these days.'

'Does he have any birthmarks, or old fractures, anything along those lines?'

Sally nodded her head. 'He broke his right wrist falling off a rope swing when he was nine. He was a total daredevil in the days, before, well, you know what I was going to say, before the crash. He's been a lot more risk-averse since then. It makes sense when you think about it.'

Kesey nodded twice. 'Is there anything else you think I need to know about before we bring the interview to a close? Think carefully. Take as long as you need.'

Sally thought for a moment, searching her mind. 'Harry's easily led, impressionable, I think that's a fair way of putting it. It wouldn't take much to push him in one direction or another. I don't think I'm speaking out of turn.'

Kesey made some final notes before closing her pocketbook, marking the page with one of several large paperclips she always kept handy. 'Okay, thank you, Sally, that's all really helpful. I'll notify Harry as missing and get the description circulated as soon as we're finished here. From what you've told me, he's classified as a vulnerable adult. I'll ensure his case is given the priority it deserves. I'll have one of my officers check the CCTV for the area for the relevant time, and we'll make appropriate enquiries. If Harry went into town on the Friday morning as his student friend claims, someone must have seen him. That will be a good starting point. And we'll check with the local hospitals, just as a precaution, you understand. It's essential we cover all the bases. It's a well-established protocol that's there for a reason.' She checked the time, mentally rescheduling what was left of the day. 'And I'll make a few calls. That's something I can do myself.'

Sally manufactured a thin smile which disappeared as quickly as it appeared. 'Thank you, Laura. Thank you so very much. I really appreciate your help.'

'That's what I'm here for.' Kesey took a single sheet of A4 paper from a drawer and pushed it across the table, followed by a pen. 'If you could write your full name, address and contact details on there for me, that will save us a bit of time. I'll also need the details of all of Harry's friends. If you know the telephone numbers, they'd be helpful too. Someone's going to know something. The more information you can give me, the better.'

Sally spent the next five minutes or so writing out the required information, or at least that of which she was aware, in large bold capitals that she thought the detective couldn't fail to read. Where she was unsure of a number, she checked it on her smartphone and then continued. 'Right, I think that's everything.'

Kesey folded the sheet of paper in two, placing it between the pages of her pocketbook for safekeeping. She so wanted to offer reassurance, to put the poor woman at ease, but there was only so much she could say. 'As soon as I've got any news, I'll be in touch.'

'You will find him, won't you, Laura?'

'All I can do is repeat myself. We're going to do everything we can to find your son. I'll manage the investigation personally. I think of you as a friend. I won't leave any stone unturned. That I can promise you.'

Sally stood on shaky legs, gripping the table's edge as they threatened to collapse under her. 'Thank you, Laura, you've been brilliant. I can't tell you how grateful I am. It's a huge relief that you're taking the situation as seriously as you so obviously are.'

Kesey pushed back her seat. 'Try not to worry too much, Sally. Thousands of people are reported missing in the UK every year. Most of them turn up unharmed in the end.'

The colour drained from Sally's face. 'But not all of them?'

Kesey paused, wishing she hadn't said anything at all. 'No, not all of them. Some people we can't find, and some don't want to be found, that's the truth of it. But they're in the minority. We're moving quickly. It's a small town with a relatively small population. Most people are going to want to help. They always do. And those things are in our favour. They're to our advantage. I know nothing I can tell you is going to stop you worrying. I'd be the same in your place. But the chances of finding your son are far better than average.'

Sally stopped mid-step on approaching the door. 'Let's hope so. Harry's all I've got left. I couldn't bear to lose him. I'm begging you, Laura. Find my son.'

12

The heat of the early summer sun was replaced by constant drizzle seven days after Harry's enforced arrival at the compound. It swept in from the south in sheets, soaking everything in its path, as Baptist led Harry towards the community's communal meeting room, located in an area of mature trees behind the men's shared sleeping quarters.

It seemed all the members of the community were ready and waiting, seated in neat rows and facing a stage, as the big man opened the double doors and shoved Harry into the room, making him trip and lose his balance. But waiting for what? That's what Harry asked himself when he'd regained his footing. He didn't have the slightest clue. But it wouldn't be good. Of that, he was sure. Nothing about the community was ever good. Or at least nothing he'd seen or heard so far. Hopefully, some other poor sod wasn't about to get a beating. That would be far too much to bear.

Harry had never wanted a tablet more as he glanced around the room. The need for a mind-levelling chemical hit was eating away at him, the longing dominating and overwhelming almost every thought in his head. He'd pleaded, he'd begged, but with no positive result. Baptist didn't want to hear his appeals, however emotional, however earnest or heartfelt. The big man had just given that same infuriatingly predictable reply with a blank look on his bearded face: 'Have faith, newbie. How many times do I have to tell you? God is all the medicine you need.' Baptist had said it, and he'd repeated it, time and again until Harry almost believed it himself. But if God was to ease his suffering, it hadn't happened yet. Harry's mind was flooded with self-doubt as he looked around him, a negative wave of dark thoughts that further sapped his flagging morale, a black dog of depression beating him down a little further.

Cold turkey was agonising, horrific, the worst thing in the world. *Maybe I'm not praying hard enough. Perhaps my faith isn't strong enough.* That's what Baptist had claimed, oh so insistently, before slapping him, before knocking him to the floor and pinning him there as he'd struggled to free himself to no avail. Whatever the cause of his escalating suffering, it seemed it was his fault and his alone. He'd brought it on himself. It was no more than he deserved. The big man had driven it home. Shouted it up close, warm spittle spraying from his mouth, impossible to ignore. He had to learn to trust in God's good grace. Do that, that one simple thing and all would be sweetness and light. Would it? Really? Would it? Or would his life continue to disintegrate? That seemed far more likely.

Harry stood in trepidation, mind still racing, lungs expanded, and pupils enlarged, attention intensely focussed on his own survival. He noticed that he was sweating despite the cooler temperature and damp patches were forming under both his arms. Harry didn't want to be drawn in as every eye in the room turned to stare, seemingly focussed on him and only him. Everyone continued watching as Baptist led him between the rows of seats towards the front row, just a few feet from the stage, with its spotlights, white cotton backdrop, polished chrome microphone stand, and large, bespoke black wooden speakers to each side, facing outward towards the gathering. Baptist sat himself down in one of two free seats located to the side of the aisle close to the centre point of the stage and pulled Harry down next to him.

They sat there in silence along with the others for another twenty minutes or so, until that same trumpet fanfare suddenly soared out from the two speakers, filling the room with vibrating sound that sent a shockwave of excitement around the crowd.

Harry looked around him as the lights dimmed, leaving the brightly lit stage as the centre of attention. The wave of delight continued to build, reaching a point of virtual ecstasy as the brass fanfare slowly faded away to silence, signalling their master's imminent arrival. Cameron strolled out onto the stage only seconds later. He looked out on his congregation, beaming, as his appearance was met by a cacophony of yelps, cheers, screeches and feverish clapping, that got louder and louder as he drank it all in, feeding his ego, wallowing in their veneration, and loving every single moment, as his self-worth soared.

Vincent Cameron stood there on chubby legs, waving, smiling, feeling he may actually explode with the joy of it all. He continued milking the applause until he thought the time to address his flock precisely right.

You could have heard a pin drop as Cameron raised an open hand in the air while gripping the microphone tightly with the other. He held it three inches from his mouth and began, 'Thank you, my children, your warm and friendly greeting is to your credit. We reap what we sow both in this life and the next. God will reward you for your loyalty and devotion. Welcome, my children. Welcome to our weekly healing service. Great things will happen if you trust in your faith. Shout out your praise!'

Cameron placed the microphone back on its metal stand,

looking out on the white-clad gathering, waiting for the inevitable response, holding a hand to his ear. The chanting started with the children in high, chirpy voices, followed by the women, and finally, the men, whose loud shouts drowned out the sound of the others. 'The master is great. I am nothing. All praise to the master. The master is great. I am nothing. All praise to the master!'

Cameron allowed the zealous chanting to continue for another five minutes or so before finally raising a hand to silence his congregation. The room was quiet in seconds, as the gathering eagerly awaited their master's words of wisdom.

'Thank you, my children. God has heard you. You are blessed. We are His chosen people. Never forget that. Now is a time for healing!' He allowed time for the inevitable cheers of delight and then raised a hand for a second time. 'I have grave news, my children. God has spoken to me! He is looking down and weeping. Not all of you are free of sin. Some have doubts when they should have certainty.' He waited for the resulting boos to subside. 'Others have dark thoughts, thoughts of disobedience and self-interest when only the needs of God and our faithful community should concern them!' The boos began again, louder this time, each member of the community searching their troubled minds, desperately hoping they wouldn't be singled out. Worried that their master's wrath may fall on them and strike them down.

Cameron looked about him, taking pleasure in the gathering's growing distress for a time, and then shouting, 'Silence!'

The response was instant, allowing him to continue, this time in hushed tones as if he were sharing a secret for only them to hear. 'Your sins have allowed the devil and all his vile demons to attack your minds and bodies. Did you hear me, my children? Any illness you may suffer, any aches and pains, any fever or disability, is the work of Beelzebub. The lord of the flies! Your immoral acts, your evil wrongdoings, give the devil strength! Did you hear what I said to you, my children? It is essential that you confess your sins. Every single one of you must beg for God's forgiveness. Ask Him to protect you from the devil's dark attentions. Call out to Him in faith, praise be, praise be! Pray to God for forgiveness and healing, my children. If you have sufficient faith, He will heal all.' And then a line with which Harry was entirely familiar. 'God is all the medicine you need.'

Every member of the community fell to their knees, Harry included, as he followed their lead. They clasped their hands together in front of them, heads bowed, eyes tightly shut, and prayed. They pleaded for forgiveness and gave thanks for God's mercy. They asked for healing, for whatever ailment they suffered or feared. And some questioned the strength of their faith. They pleaded pardon for what they saw as their almost infinite failings. Their master had said it loud and clear. If they were ill in body, mind or spirit, it was their own fault. They'd brought it on themselves. It was down to them.

Cameron paced the stage, first one way and then the other, occasionally stopping to shout out words of encouragement or condemnation, until he finally tired of the spectacle a short time later. He moved to the very front of the stage, just a few feet from Harry's seat, and called out, 'Up you get, my children. Get off your knees and return to your seats. God has heard you. The spirit is moving amongst us. Some of you are being healed right now!' He waited for the inevitable cheers to abate before continuing. 'Can you feel God's healing hand touching you, my children? Can you feel the heat as it penetrates your mind, body and soul? Because I can, I can! Our glorious God is driving the cancerous cells from your bodies. He's healing you of whatever ailment the devil inflicted in his hateful vindictiveness. Praise be, my children. All praise to God. That's it, on your feet, throw your arms in the air and worship. Shout out for all to hear. Proclaim your faith. Praise be! Nothing is beyond God's power.'

Cameron waited for the resulting frenzy to reach fever pitch, before deciding the time was precisely right. He looked down at Baptist, meeting the big man's eyes, and nodding. Baptist responded immediately, taking Harry by the arm and leading him up three wooden steps to their left, behind the curtain and directly onto the stage. Harry repeatedly blinked, eyelids twitching as the spotlight dazzled him, making him wince. He stood there in apprehension, open-mouthed and emotional, as the gathered congregation continued to worship as if as one, shouting out their praise.

Cameron took the microphone in hand, lifting it to his face as Baptist manoeuvred Harry to the centre point of the stage, where he stopped. 'Silence, my children, be seated. God has heard you. It is time for quiet contemplation. He has miracles to perform.'

The anticipation was almost touchable as Cameron turned towards Harry, taking his hot and sweaty hand in his, as Baptist took a backward step. 'Look at this your new brother, my children. Look at him and witness God's majesty.' He placed an open hand on top of Harry's wavering head, spreading his fingers wide and pressing down. 'I have a truly inspirational tale of miraculous transformation to share with you, my children. When this creature of God arrived with us, he was paralysed by mental illness born of the devil. Shadow's mind was poisoned by the dark forces of hell. Our brother was worthless, of no use to himself or anybody else, a pitiful creature devoid of virtue!' Cameron paused as a series of boos and jeers rang out. 'But look at him now, my children. He is transformed! Feast your eyes. Witness God's infinite power. Shadow's mind is healed! Shout out your praise, my children. He is a new and beautiful creation! Only God could work such wonders. He works through me in mysterious ways that are beyond mere human comprehension. Release your faith, my children. Shout out your praise!'

Cameron's pronouncements were met by a wave of elated calls and cheers that rang out, getting louder and louder as some members of the gathering entered a trance-like state, increasingly suggestible, their consciousness fragile. Just for a brief instant, Harry felt inclined to join in, to belong. To cheer and shout out with the others. A part of him wanted to believe it was real. That his sceptical doubts were misguided. That his traumatised mind was no longer troubled by the past. Could it be true? Really? It could be, couldn't it, if one embraced the possibility? Harry saw his father's reassuringly familiar face in his mind's eye, but it faded all too quickly when Cameron spoke again, breaking his focus.

'Silence, my children. Enough! It is time to watch and listen in quiet reverence. Time to witness God's infinite healing powers. Focus on your faith, my children. The spirit is amongst us. God has another miracle to perform.'

The entire congregation inched forwards. They were keen to see something of which they'd heard, something spectacular, something dramatic and transformative. Desperate not to miss anything.

'Our new brother has toiled hard for us, my children. He's worked in the vegetable garden, he's planted, he's weeded, and he's picked God's generous bounty to feed us all, with the loving guidance of his supervisors. I'm delighted to tell you that Shadow has settled in better than any of us could have hoped. He has quickly become a valued member of our small community. And now, God will reward him for his loyalty.'

Cameron took Harry's hand in his and began walking him along the stage, first one way and then the other, like a prize bull at a county show. 'Shadow has a chronic limp. He was born with one leg shorter than the other.' He ushered Harry further along the stage, stopped, and then started again in the opposite direction, shoving him forwards and making him stumble. 'Can you see it, my children? Shadow can't walk with confidence. He loses his balance, he stalls, and he falls. Such a sad state to behold. Look at our brother, my children. Can you see the devil's work?'

'Yes, yes, yes! Heal him! Heal him! God is great. All praise to the master! Praise be, praise be!'

Cameron pushed Harry to the floor, instructing him to lie still and not to move until told.

'Look at your brother, my children. Focus on healing. Release your faith to the universe. Without God's spiritual help, Shadow's disability will only get worse. Very soon he wouldn't be able to walk at all. He'd end up in a wheelchair, unable to perform even the simplest of daily tasks to an acceptable level. Can God help him, my children? Can God undo the devil's work? Is your faith strong enough?'

'Yes, yes, yes! Heal him! Heal him! God is great. All praise to the master. Praise be, praise be! All praise to the master!'

Cameron then took each of Harry's ankles in hand, as Baptist switched on a nearby camera, projecting a large, close-up image of events on the white cloth backdrop for all to see. Cameron pulled on Harry's right ankle, extending his leg while pushing up on the left. 'Our brother's leg is growing, my children! It is lengthening right now to match the other! Can you see it? Is your faith strong enough? It's a divine miracle, my children. A wondrous and supernatural phenomenon science couldn't begin to explain. Look, my children, look! Bear witness to God's glorious majesty.'

A thick swathe of worshippers crowded around the stage now, pushing, squeezing forward, eager for a closer view, as the younger children clung to one person or another, hanging onto legs and arms. Everyone shouted out. Everyone chanted. 'Yes, yes, yes! God is great! Heal him, heal him! All praise to the master!'

Cameron helped Harry to his feet, holding the microphone close to his lips. 'Can you feel any pain, my child?'

'No!'

'You're not feeling any pain at all?'

Harry hadn't felt any in the first place, but for the moment that fact didn't register. He experienced a surge of unfamiliar emotion that was entirely new to him, a high of sorts, as the cheers continued to ring out. 'None!'

'Bend down, my child. Bend down and touch your toes.'

Harry had always been flexible, naturally, without the need to stretch. He bent easily at the waist, placing the palms of both hands flat on the stage, as Cameron shouted his enthusiastic approval.

'Jump up and down, my child. You are healed. Show everyone how well your new leg works. Give thanks for your miracle. Show God your gratitude. Sing His praise!'

Harry began jumping on the spot, lowering himself to the floor, squatting on his haunches and then leaping up, throwing his arms in the air and yelling, more noise than words. His heart raced as blood rushed to his muscles, adrenaline altering his metabolism in a rush of overwhelming sensation.

Cameron stood back and watched the spectacle unfolding before him, feeling a potent mix of excitement and delight as his confidence soared to a new and dramatic high. He looked out at his adoring followers, and then at Harry, who had slowed now but was still jumping. The self-proclaimed master looked from one scene to the other and had never felt more powerful. He congratulated himself on his performance, silently proclaiming himself the chosen one, the new Messiah, the very greatest amongst men. A wondrous future stretched out before him in his mind's eye, playing like a cinematic film in which he starred.

Yes, yes, he was meant to take advantage of the plebs. Intended to mess with their ordinary lives for his own satisfaction. They were his playthings, unimportant but amusing, every single one of them. But how far could he take it? That was the real question. *How far? How far? Oh, well, there is only one way to find out. Push it to the limit.* That made sense. *The domination of my inferiors is my birth right, my fundamental right.* He repeated it and believed it, with no room for doubt.

Cameron beckoned to a slight, twelve-year-old girl with short mousy hair cropped into a bob, who was standing to the left of the crowd, arms in the air, cheering along with the rest.

He reached out, guiding her up the steps, onto the stage, and finally behind the curtain and out of the building, through a rear door restricted for his exclusive use. He could still hear the gathering's excited yelps and cheers of praise as he rushed the whimpering child towards his private quarters, a short walk away in the fading light of the evening. He smiled as he opened his bedroom door, shoving her into the room, and gave a loud squeal of satisfaction as she fell sideways onto the bed.

Vincent Cameron loomed over his latest victim, large and threatening as he began removing his damp robes, cackling like a demented hyena with every move of his body. How far could he take it? How far? He laughed again, head back, overhanging belly fat wobbling like a birthday jelly, as she began to weep, warm and salty tears rolling down her pallid face. Why on earth had he ever created such self-imposed limits in the first place? That's what he asked himself, as she continued to shiver and shake. There was no need for self-control, no need for limitations. The laws of the land didn't apply, not to him, not now, not ever. It was the only logical conclusion he could reach. The only thing that made any sense to him as he stared down at her with bulging eyes. Cameron urged himself on as he climbed onto the bed, one stiff limb at a time.

Limitations were for ordinary people, for lesser men. *I am above all that, special. I can get away with almost anything.*

13

Detective Inspector Laura Kesey ran a brush through her short, wavy brown hair, checked what she liked to think was her subtle lipstick in a hand mirror taken from her bag, and then strode purposefully down the long, well-lit corridor leading to Chief Superintendent Nigel Halliday's office door, on the third floor of the modernist concrete building. Kesey silently acknowledged that she was feeling a bit like a child anticipating an unwelcome meeting with a teacher, as she slowed and paused next to a recently installed, plastic drinking fountain. Why the nerves? She wasn't really sure. The meeting wasn't a particularly big deal. It only involved providing an update on what seemed a routine case. *Oh shit! I want to impress the new boss a little too much for my own good.*

Kesey filled a paper cup to the halfway point and raised it to her lips, still deep in thought as she sipped the chilled water, wetting her mouth. What was it about Halliday that set her teeth on edge? He had plonker written all over him. Or was she making assumptions she wasn't entitled to make? Jumping to conclusions, suppositions based on very little evidence at all?

Perhaps she should give him the benefit of the doubt before deciding if she liked him. First impressions weren't always accurate, after all. And she had to admit that he appeared reasonably approachable in a self-important, senior officer, posh boy sort of way. Yeah, but did he have the hard-won frontline experience that earned respect, the hours pounding the beat? That's what really mattered. Or was he all paper qualifications and accelerated promotion, the sort of officer most subordinates loathed with a vengeance, and for excellent reasons, too? She'd heard rumours of a PhD, of time spent studying at Cambridge University. Gossip maybe, but gossip could be accurate.

She couldn't imagine ever getting on with a man like that, given her more humble background and rise up the ranks, but she had to try. West Wales was a relatively small force with a limited number of senior positions, and, therefore, limited opportunities for promotion. There was little point in alienating a man who'd inevitably play a significant role in deciding her future career path. Not before she gave him a fair chance.

He was the boss, like it or not, and she just had to make the best of it. He held all the cards, all the aces. How did the old saying go? 'God, please grant me the wisdom to accept the things I cannot change.' It was something along those lines. The Bible, maybe? Or Shakespeare? Well, whoever had said it had never said a truer word.

Kesey checked her make-up for one final time before knocking on a light oak-veneered door emblazoned with Halliday's name and rank, as if anyone needed reminding. She stood there, tapping a foot against the floor until he called her in via the speaker system. Kesey walked into the recently appointed head of the criminal investigation department's excessively large office, to find him standing at a picture window with a sweeping view of the pleasant market town of Carmarthen and the green hills beyond. Halliday turned to face her after what felt like an age, reaching out a hand in greeting, gripping Kesey's a little too firmly for her liking, crushing her fingers.

'DI Kesey, isn't it?'

Kesey changed her stance. 'Yes, sir, Laura Kesey. We were introduced by the chief constable when you first arrived. You told me you'd transferred from the Met in the hope of a quieter life. You said you wanted to make a difference.'

'Ah, yes, you replaced the infamous DI Gravel that I've been told so much about. He seems to be something of a local legend.'

Kesey nodded. 'Yeah, that's right, he was one of life's good guys, the best. I still miss him. He's not an easy man to forget. He taught me a great deal about being a good detective.'

Halliday sat himself down behind a meticulously ordered Victorian desk, perched on a black leather swivel chair, and indicated to Kesey to take a seat opposite him. Her seat was smaller and lower than his.

'I'm glad to hear it, Laura. Hopefully, you can put that advice to good use. Now, tell me. What can I do for you?'

Kesey glanced at the numerous framed academic certificates hanging on the wall behind him and rolled her eyes. Why display the frigging things? No one likes a show-off. Maybe she should trust her gut. It seemed her initial instincts had been correct all along. 'I wanted to update you on the Gilmore case, sir, the missing university student.'

'Very well, Laura, I'm all ears.'

Kesey thought she'd detected a hint of sarcasm in his tone, but she continued, nonetheless. 'Initial enquiries suggest it may be a more complex case than it first appeared.'

'Get to the point, Laura. I haven't got all day.'

She bit the inside of her lower lip hard. 'I'd appreciate you signing off more overtime, sir. I'd like to dedicate two additional detectives to the case for as long as it takes.'

Halliday pushed up the sleeve of his bespoke Savile Row jacket, checking his watch, making it obvious. Off-the-peg items just didn't meet his required standards. 'I usually have a cup of tea at about this time, diary allowing. Will you join me?'

'Um, yeah, yeah, I don't see why not? I'm always up for a cuppa.'

He pointed to his right. 'You'll find everything you need on the tray over there, inspector. I take mine black with no sugar. Tea shouldn't be drunk any other way. That's what my dear mama used to tell me. We can continue talking while the water comes to the boil.'

Kesey switched on the kettle and began preparing the tea, quietly seething, speaking without turning to face him. 'Like I said, I'm going to need a bigger budget for the case. And I'd like your agreement to go public with an appeal for information. Something on the Welsh radio and TV. I'm beginning to think we may be dealing with an abduction of some kind. As you know, Gilmore was seen being placed in a white Transit van. I've established that a vehicle with a similar description was linked to the disappearance of a twenty-two-year-old woman in December last year in the South Wales Police area. Her body was found in the River Taff two months later.'

'Murder?'

'The body was too badly degraded to establish a cause of death, but foul play was strongly suspected.'

'Did South Wales get anywhere with it?'

'No, an elderly witness provided a vague description of the suspect vehicle, and nothing more. It's enough to raise our concern, but it doesn't help us.'

'There are some biscuits in the drawer if you fancy one.'

Kesey dropped tea bags into two porcelain cups, poured the boiling water, and finally added a drop of milk for herself. 'Not for me, thanks, I'm in training. I've still got a couple of pounds to lose. Shall I bring the packet?'

Halliday shook his head. 'Training? Training for what?'

She handed him his cup before returning to her seat. 'I'm a kick-boxing instructor. I made the British team. I'll be fighting in the European championships in September.'

'As long as it doesn't interfere with your duties.'

Kesey raised an eyebrow. 'It won't.'

'I'm glad to hear it, Laura. Now, let's get back to business. Tell me more about this case of yours. It sounds like the sort of thing we'd have dealt with without too much trouble in the Met, but I suppose we'd better treat it seriously. It's what we're paid for after all.'

Kesey shook her head, frowning. 'I used to think much the same way when I first moved here from the West Midlands force. I really thought I'd made the biggest mistake of my life. But I was wrong. Crime is crime, sir. The figures are lower here, of course they are, that goes without saying, but there's fewer officers to deal with it too. And the offences are no less serious. It's police work, just like in the big city.'

Halliday appeared less than impressed. 'If you say so, inspector, if you say so, now let's focus back on the case. You have my attention. I suggest you take full advantage. We can indulge a theoretical discussion at a more appropriate time.'

Sarky bastard. 'Harry Gilmore has been missing for ten days with no sightings, no phone use and no cash withdrawals. It's as if he's disappeared off the face of the earth.'

He wanted to laugh. He so wanted to laugh. 'We're talking about an adult, yes? Am I missing something?'

'He's a local lad, he's vulnerable, and his disappearance is totally out of character. I believe we've got good cause to be concerned.'

'Vulnerable, how?'

'Gilmore suffers depression, sir. I've spoken to his mother. His medication was found in his student lodgings. It's not likely he's coping without it.'

'Suicide?'

'I really don't think so.'

Halliday nodded. 'I'm assuming you've contacted local hospitals and the like?'

'We have, and no, nothing.'

He drained his cup, resting his elbows on his desk, revealing solid gold cufflinks that gleamed as a shaft of bright sunshine broke through the clouds, flooding the room with light. 'I understand your concerns, really I do, but nothing you've said so far tells me the case is anything close to as heinous as your earlier comments suggested. It's important not to go over the top, Laura. It's essential to remain objective. Gilmore may well have gone off somewhere in this van of his own volition. It wouldn't be surprising if you think about it logically. It's likely he isn't even aware anyone's looking for him. Talk of kidnapping and murder seems a little excessive at this stage, don't you think?'

Kesey felt her entire body tense. 'We've reviewed the CCTV for the relevant time, sir. Gilmore is seen being helped into a white van by a young female and an older, much larger male.'

'Helped?'

'It looks as if he was either totally inebriated or drugged.'

'But you used the word *helped*, not forced? That strongly suggests doubts on your part. I'm not in a position to waste resources for you or anybody else.'

Kesey emitted a long, deep, audible breath. 'Perhaps *helped* wasn't the best choice of words.'

'You must learn to be more specific, Laura. I shouldn't need to tell you that. You're a DI now, and you need to conduct yourself accordingly.'

Kesey rubbed the back of her neck, her hand moving in jerks. She rushed her reply. The words spilling from her mouth. 'Gilmore was picked up by the large male and physically placed into the rear of the vehicle. That is clearly recorded on film and has been confirmed by a witness. She got the distinct impression that he wasn't co-operating with the process. The same man, the driver, shouted out, claiming it was Gilmore's birthday, which clearly wasn't true. Why would he lie if his motives weren't criminal?'

'Is the witness credible?'

'She's a local primary school teacher, a woman in her thirties.'

'That doesn't necessarily mean anything.'

The DI cleared her throat. 'I've viewed the tape myself, sir, and yes, she's credible. It looks like an abduction to me.'

'Very well, Laura. Have we got the vehicle's index number?'

Kesey looked past him, at one framed certificate or another, BA, MA, PhD, rather than meet his eyes. 'There's nothing helpful on CCTV, nothing clear enough to be of any use to us, but Tanya, one of our probationary constables, stopped a vehicle meeting the description on the M4 near Cross Hands that same afternoon.'

'Do the times fit?'

'Yeah, they do. I've checked, twice, that's one hundred per cent certain. And her description of the driver matches the man seen transferring Gilmore into the vehicle earlier in the day. Our suspect was accompanied by two females, who like him were dressed entirely in white. Tanya has confirmed they were sitting in the front seats of the van along with the driver.'

'Entirely in white?'

'Yes, sir, that's what I said, white.'

'Strange.'

'It could be some sort of hippy set-up. There's several communes in the area.'

'Are you saying that with any degree of certainty?'

'No, I'm saying it could be. That's all, it could be.'

Halliday looked at Kesey with a pinched expression, as if she'd emitted a bad smell, stinking the place out. 'Try to stick to the facts, Laura. Assumption is never a good thing in our line of work.'

'I'll keep it in mind.'

'Okay, let's move on... why did this constable you mentioned stop the vehicle in the first place?'

'A minor road traffic offence.'

'That was fortuitous.'

Kesey nodded. 'Yeah, it was. It may have given us the break we needed.'

'Was there any sign of Gilmore?'

'If he was still in the back of the van, which seems likely, there's no way Tanya could have seen him.'

Halliday pulled his head back. 'What the hell's that supposed to mean? She could have looked. She could have opened the rear doors. That seems blatantly obvious. Did the stupid girl not think of searching?'

Kesey was quick to reply. 'Oh, come on, boss. Why would she? She knew nothing of any possible abduction at that stage. She talked to the driver about a faulty exhaust, and that was all. Why on earth would she look in the back of the van? I'm certain you wouldn't have done any different in her place.'

'I'm not so sure. Maybe she's not up to the job. You said she's a probationer. It could be time to let her go.'

'Tanya's a good officer. The last thing she needs is a senior officer casting doubts on her ability without good reason. She's shown a lot of potential. We'd do well to hang on to her.'

His blank expression became a sneer. 'Well, if she's as good as you say she is, no doubt she'll have checked the driver's documents, yes?'

Now Kesey knew she didn't like him. Not one little bit. She was beginning to think Halliday was a misogynist, a woman-hater, the kind of man she'd encountered all too often on both sides of the law. 'Yeah, she did, as it happens. And she made a written record of the index number, as good officers do. The vehicle is registered to a Michael Richardson in the Didsbury area. The Greater Manchester Police paid him a visit for me. He sold the van for cash just over a year ago, but he hadn't bothered submitting any paperwork to the DVLA. The buyer meets the description of our suspect, white-skinned, six feet four or five inches, heavily built with a West Country accent. It was the same man, all right. That's one assumption I'm very happy to make.'

'But we haven't got a name?'

'No, the details given to Tanya were false. No surprises there. I wasn't expecting anything else.'

Halliday picked up a blue cardboard file, his reading glasses balanced on the very tip of his nose. 'I think I've heard enough, Laura, you seem to be managing the case reasonably well up to this point. I suggest you get on with it.'

'What about my overtime budget?'

He opened the file, head down, shuffling through a thick sheaf of papers to little if any apparent effect. 'Put something in writing, Inspector. And have it on my desk by three o'clock this afternoon. I'll try to read it before the end of the day.'

'And the media coverage?'

'I'll give it some thought.'

'I've got a slot booked on the Radio Wales news at four today in Cardiff. Should I go ahead?'

Halliday pushed his paperwork aside. 'It would have been nice to be consulted before now.'

'Should I go ahead with it or not? Yes or no. The clock's ticking.'

He waited for a full five seconds before answering. 'Well, I can't see any reason why not. There may be some advantage in making the investigation public. But you'll need to find the boy quickly once it's done. Any failure to do so would reflect badly on the force. And on you too, of course. We're measured by our results. It's the way of the world. Failure wouldn't do your career any favours at all.'

Kesey rose to her feet. 'Is there a problem, sir?'

'A problem? What do you mean by that precisely?'

Kesey's irritation was betrayed by her face. 'Oh, you know exactly what I'm talking about. Have you got an issue with me? That's what I'm asking you. Have I said or done something to upset you, that I'm not aware of? Because it seems that way to me.'

He rose to his full height. 'I hope you're not going to be one of those overly emotional women who crumble under the slightest pressure.'

She glared at him, eyes cold and flinty. 'I'm sure we'll get on famously.'

'I'm glad to hear it, inspector. Police work isn't suited to people of a sensitive disposition.'

Kesey turned to walk away, swallowing her words. 'One last thing before you go, Laura.'

She turned to face him. 'Yeah, what is it?'

'My secretary's on maternity leave, one of the many complexities of employing females of a certain age. I'd be grateful if you'd wash the cups before you go.'

'Wash the cups? Is this a wind-up?'

'Not at all, I've never been more serious.'

Kesey pictured herself punching him, bang, right on the point of the chin. 'Oh, I don't think so, chief superintendent. I think you'll find I'm a detective, not a skivvy. I suggest you roll your sleeves up and do the job yourself.'

14

Baptist led Harry down a short, dimly lit corridor, lined with three dark-oak doors to either side. Harry had no idea where he was being taken, but the uncertainty wasn't causing him a great deal of worry, despite recent events.

Baptist had been in a surprisingly positive mood, cheerful when he'd collected him from the men's dormitory at just after 7 p.m. that evening. Harry had asked for an explanation, but it was refused with a smile. A seemingly genuine smile of something close to affection. It had helped Harry relax in a way that wouldn't have been likely only hours before. Maybe the effects of drug withdrawal were finally wearing off. Or perhaps he was starting to get used to life in the community. Harry wasn't sure which hypothesis applied, but he did know he was feeling better. He was one of them now, not an outsider, and that had its advantages. It felt good to belong.

Now, as they stopped outside the final door on the right of the corridor, Harry was feeling strangely elated, the trepidation of the recent past replaced by hope. The healing service had been the turning point. Harry had felt like a star on that stage. He'd been the centre of attention, cheered and applauded for the first time in his life. It had felt good, really good, life-affirming even. And he'd received a great deal of praise as the week went on. He'd found he liked gardening and other physical tasks much more than he'd ever thought possible.

A part of him still wanted out of there. To go home. To get back to his old life. To see his loving mum. But it felt less urgent now. It would happen, of course it would, one day. That's what he told himself. It was just a matter of time. It would happen when the moment was right. And in the interim, he could learn. He could grow. Maybe the master really was a miracle worker with a direct line to God. Why not hang around awhile and find out the truth? Why not take full advantage of the opportunities membership of the community provided? Not everyone was nearly as fortunate.

'Right then, newbie, this is it. Are you ready?'

Harry looked up at Baptist with a puzzled expression. 'Ready for what? Am I finally to have a one-to-one audience with the master? You've said I've done well. Is that what's happening here?'

Baptist laughed, head back, long greying hair falling down his back in a tangled web. 'No, you're not quite ready for that privilege, but it is good news. Our glorious master has proclaimed that your efforts on the community's behalf are worthy of reward. What you are about to receive is a gift, not an entitlement. Accept the master's kindness with a spirit of acceptance and gratitude.'

Harry stood back, wide-eyed, as Baptist opened the door. The big man moved aside for Harry to enter the room first.

'In you go, newbie. Come on, in you go. It's all good. There's nothing to be frightened of. This may well turn out to be the best night of your life.'

Harry entered a candlelit room that smelt of jasmine blended with a hint of lavender. It reminded him of his mum's house. There was a double bed at the centre of the room, clothed in white silk sheets and plump pillows covered in the same natural material. There were bright red rose petals sprinkled over the bed and on the polished hardwood floor, and a second closed door to the left side of the bed, which Harry surmised led to a bathroom.

The bedroom seemed so much more opulent than Harry's communal dormitory, so much more comfortable, so luxurious by comparison. Like another world entirely, a world of gifts that delighted the senses. Harry looked about him, grinning like a Cheshire cat, appreciating both the floral scent filling his nostrils and the visual luxury of it all. He felt like a child anticipating a treat from a trusted loved one as he turned to Baptist, his mind filled with questions that spilt from his mouth one after another, leaving no room for a reply. 'Won't I be sleeping in the dorm any more? Does everyone get their own room in time? Why the candles? Why the rose petals? Is it because I've done well? Is this room for me?'

The big man held a hand up at shoulder level, palm outwards, fingers spread wide. 'Wow, slow down, newbie. It's not your room. Or at least, not for the long term. And anyway, this isn't about the room. It's a lot better than that. The master has granted you a blessing. Not everyone is as fortunate. Sit on the bed and be patient. All is about to become clear.'

Harry sat as instructed, his heart pounding in his chest, the anticipation almost too much for him to bear as the second door slowly opened to the sound of an opera aria, sung by a woman. He'd heard it somewhere before, but couldn't think where.

And then as Harry stared, wide-eyed, at the slowly opening door, Achara appeared, smiling seductively, moving with sensual grace, looking even more beautiful than when he'd met her on that first memorable day, if such a thing were possible. She was still dressed in white, but it was white silk now, which, Harry happily noted, clung to her curves like a second skin. Achara sat on the bed next to him, still not speaking, but appearing confident and relaxed. As if she wanted to be there. As if she were looking forward to whatever the night may bring.

Baptist stood in front of them, close to the exit, looking from one to the other, moving his head stiffly, reading their body language, studying the expressions on their faces. 'Our esteemed master is allowing you some time together as a reward for your loyalty and good works. I will leave you shortly and will not return until morning. Now, lie back and try to relax. Sex is a gift from God. Talk, get to know each other a little better, and then do whatever feels right. The spirit will guide you if you have sufficient faith. You will not be interrupted or disturbed until I return in the light of dawn.'

Achara moved easily, crossing her legs under her, slender shoulders straight and back. She looked up at Baptist and smiled, eyes twinkling in the light of the flickering flames. 'God is great. All praise to the master.'

Harry felt inclined to join in as Baptist called out his enthusiastic response, whooping, hollering, 'Yes, yes, yes! Praise be! Praise be! Call out your worship for all of God's saints to hear! Drive the devil out! Send him back from whence he came.'

All three chanted in unison for another five minutes, before Baptist finally shouted, 'Enough! God has heard us. All praise to the master.' He turned his back and left the room without another word.

Achara placed an arm around Harry's shoulder, pulling him close. She spoke in a hushed whisper, her warm, minty breath caressing his face. 'It's lovely to see you again, Harry. Or should I call you Shadow? It's your new name, after all. Do you like it? I'm certain the master gave it to you for a great reason. Tell me what you think.'

'Um, yeah, having a new name still seems a bit strange, but I guess I'm happy with either Harry or Shadow, it's up to you.'

'Then Shadow it is. God chose the name, and our leader gave it to you. It's who you are now. Accept and embrace your new identity. And I need you to understand that you can tell me absolutely anything while we're together. I want you to share your innermost thoughts.' She touched his thigh, lingering. 'If we're going to share our bodies, we have to share our minds first, that's true intimacy. If you can't trust me, then who?'

Harry experienced a surge of excitement, the anticipation heightening his senses. He was desperate to see her naked. Desperate to touch her soft skin. He leant into her, appreciating the warmth of her body against his. He craned his neck, trying to kiss her lips, but she turned her head away, and said, 'What's the hurry, tiger? Patience is a virtue. Let's talk awhile. We've got all night long to get to know each other properly. There are things I need to ask you first. Things I need to know. Do you trust me, or not? I need to hear you say it. The sex will be all the better for it. You won't be sorry you waited.'

Harry had never wanted something more. Seconds felt like minutes. He wanted her so very badly. 'I do trust you. Of course, I trust you.'

Achara pecked his cheek, touching his face with her tongue. 'What, even after the part I played in bringing you to this place?'

The last thing Harry wanted was to upset her. Not now, not when he was so very close to consummating their relationship. He felt driven by his hormones, supersensitive to her touch, ready to do and say almost anything to please her. 'Yes, I trust you, even after that. I think I may be falling in love.'

'That's good to hear, my brother. It's been playing on my mind. I know life here is very different from what you were used to in your previous life. It can be difficult to adapt, even for the most spiritual of people. Now, tell me, how are you finding it here? Deep down, I mean. Tell me, what do you *really* think?'

'Um, yeah, it was difficult at first. Especially after seeing what happened to River. I'd never seen anything like that before. He was beaten so very badly. I won't lie to you, it was shocking. I couldn't believe the state he was in.'

Her eyes narrowed. 'Do you think his punishment was justified?'

Harry opened his mouth to speak, but then closed it again when he couldn't find the words.

'Am I right in assuming you don't want to talk about it?'

'No, not really, you said to be honest. I can't be any more honest than that.'

'You're not going to get away with it that easily.'

Harry laughed. 'No, I thought not.'

Achara kissed his lips, brushing them with hers, gently, but still with passion. 'Then, I'll tell you what we'll do. We'll make a game of it. I'll ask you a question. And if you answer honestly, I'll take off one item of clothing. If you don't, you take one off. That seems fair. And believe me, I'll recognise the truth when I hear it. Are you up for it?'

Harry licked his top lip and smiled. 'How does the game end?'

'Oh, it ends when we're both naked. That sounds like fun, don't you think?'

'Yeah, you won't hear me arguing.'

She took off one white sock and threw it to the floor, revealing red painted toenails. 'There you go, there's your first honest answer right there. I've kept my side of the bargain.'

'I was hoping for the top.'

'Oh, yes, I bet you were. You're going to have to answer a much more difficult question for that.'

His eyes lit up. 'Ask away.'

'Do you want to go back to your old life?'

'Honestly?'

'Yes, absolutely, that's the whole point of the game.'

'I am starting to settle in here, but I still miss my mum. I worry about her sometimes. She's got absolutely no idea what happened to me. I'd like to get in touch and put her mind to rest. You know, just to say I'm okay. I'd feel a lot better if I could.'

'Would you describe where you are?'

Harry patted her leg just above the knee. 'Come on, I answered the question. Surely that's got to be worth you taking off another sock, at the very least.'

She peeled it off slowly and threw it to the floor with a graceful toss of her hand. 'Tell me, Shadow, have you tried to get hold of a phone since you've been here?'

'Yeah, I did look when I first arrived, but not since.'

Achara took off her silk blouse. She folded it and placed it on the floor next to the bed. 'Why not since?'

'Well, I've asked where mine is, but Baptist made his displeasure perfectly clear when I did. So, I haven't asked again. I guess I don't want to be punished. It really is that simple.'

'If I offered you a phone, would you use it? Would you contact your mum?'

'What about our game?'

She unfastened and removed her lacy white bra, pert breasts in full view, nipples erect. 'So, what's the answer?'

He stared at her chest and had never wanted her more. 'Yeah, I guess I would.'

Achara tensed when he touched her breast. 'Not quite yet, Shadow, you have one more question to answer. What do you think of the master?'

Harry hesitated. 'That's a difficult question to answer.'

She forced a smile. 'Ah, a less than honest reply. Now it's time for you to take something off. Come on, make your choice, I'm waiting.'

Harry removed his trousers with fumbling fingers to reveal the bulge of his cock pressing against the tight fabric of his underpants.

Achara reached across and tapped his penis, just for a fraction of a second, before withdrawing her hand and raising a finger to her lips. 'Come on, I asked you a question. You were at the miracle service. You were on the stage along with the master. You saw his unworldly powers up close and personal. Surely, you must have an opinion to share. I'd be taking my trousers off next. That would only leave my thong. The game's nearly reaching its climax. It would be a real shame to stop now.'

Harry ran his eyes over her lithe body, up, down and back again, lingering on her bare breasts, salivating. He asked himself how much to say, how much to share. 'Yeah, I was really impressed on the night. But then I thought, did I ever have a limp? You can't cure something that wasn't there in the first place. I'm not sure, that's the truth of it. Maybe I did, and maybe I didn't. I'm just not certain. It may have been a miracle, or maybe not.'

Achara's expression darkened. 'Doubts are the work of the devil.'

'I've tried praying for clarity.'

'Oh, you've prayed, have you?'

'Yes, I truly have.'

She pulled away from him, picking up her bra. 'Well, if you have prayed, it wasn't nearly hard enough!'

Harry sat up, the disappointment crushing. 'Oh, come on, Achara, you asked me for honesty. I didn't mean to spoil the mood.'

Achara reached up and pointed to the lens of a camera implanted in the dark, wooden wall, high in one corner of the room to her side of the bed. It pointed in a downward trajectory, covering the entire space. 'Can you see it, Shadow?'

Harry looked at the camera first, and then at her, confused as his world became a darker and more frightening place. All love had gone. It seemed all that was left was hate. 'Yes, I can see it, but what, err, why, I don't, I d-don't understand.'

Achara stood to the side of the bed, arms crossed, eyes cold, fixing Harry with a steely glower that made him shudder. 'Everything that you've said and done has been filmed. The master is watching and listening as we speak. You've let yourself down, Shadow. You've let yourself down in the worst possible way. All you can do now is beg for mercy. Oh dear, my brother, your life hangs by a thread.'

15

Baptist dragged Harry from the candlelit bedroom, down the corridor, out onto the concrete parade ground, and across the well-tended vegetable gardens, towards a heavily wooded area approximately 500 yards beyond the nearest community building. The big man rushed Harry along, ignoring his protestations, shoving or slapping him forcefully if he slowed, stalled or struggled. Harry asked for mercy, he begged for mercy, but Baptist didn't want to hear a single word he said.

The master's instructions had been clear. 'Put Shadow in the hole. Leave him there for seven days and tell him to pray. Tell him to pray harder than he's ever prayed before. Provide him with only limited rations once a day. If he's worthy, he will survive. And if not, he will die. The outcome will be God's will. Out of darkness comes light.'

Harry stopped struggling, resorting to pleading as Baptist grabbed his arm still tighter, digging in his fingers, making him wince. 'Please, Baptist, I'm sorry, I'm really sorry. I didn't mean what I said. I was stupid, foolish! I take it all back. Please, where are you taking me? You're frightening me, man. Please stop, I thought, I thought we were friends.'

Baptist increased his pace, striding over the uneven ground in easy bounds, pushing Harry ahead of him now, and then dragging him back by the hair when he attempted to run. 'You can shut up now, or I'll shut you up. I can hurt you if you want me to. Make your mind up. It really is up to you.'

When they eventually stopped, there was nothing out of the ordinary to see. Just a large area of unkempt grassy fields, surrounded by tall trees, silhouetted against an inky sky. But as Baptist lifted and moved two heavy turf pallets aside, a rusty steel hatch became visible in the ground, big enough for an adult to fit through with comparative ease.

Harry's bowels evacuated, loose excrement running down his legs as he stared at the metal door in the light of a half-moon partly shrouded in cloud. He flinched as an owl hooted in the distance and tried to pull away to no effect as Baptist grabbed his forearm with vice-like strength. Harry began moaning, emitting a series of low, feeble sounds, as the big man reached down, opening the hatch with one hand, while still holding his struggling prisoner with the other. Harry was met by the stomach-turning stench of decay as Baptist forced him to his knees on the very edge of the dark hole. Harry threw up, and continued heaving, as Baptist lowered him below the ground, ignoring his tearful pleading for clemency. And then, just when Harry thought things couldn't possibly get any worse, the big man dropped him. Harry fell ten feet or so and hit the damp earth hard with an audible thud, twisting an ankle and dislocating a knee with the force of the impact. He lay, shaken and bruised on the cold, wet earth, looking up at his tormentor, as he began to close the hatch. Harry screamed, 'No!' just as Baptist secured his underground cell with a large bolt and began placing the turf pallets back in place.

Harry continued to weep, warm tears welling in rapidly blinking eyes as Baptist walked away. Harry's body ached and the choking fear of claustrophobia was all-consuming, suffocating, but it was the pervasive stench of human waste that troubled him most. He sucked in the fetid air and gagged, picturing rotting flesh, flies, maggots, and desperately tried to drive the images from his mind. He began yelling out for help, pleading for mercy, for absolution, shouting Achara's name as loud as he could, calling for his mother time and again. But all was silence. Harry was alone. There was no one to alleviate his dread. No one to save him from whatever isolation would bring.

Harry lay there in the coal-black darkness, curled up on the damp earth, holding himself tightly, arms wrapped around his belly for another twenty minutes or more before finally dredging up sufficient resolve to act. He lifted himself onto all fours, attempting to ignore the stinging pain in his leg, and began crawling around the restricted space of his underground cell, one arm stretched out into the impenetrable gloom, feeling the wood-lined walls with a clammy hand, searching for anything that could provide even the slightest hope of escape and survival.

Harry struggled to his feet after about ten minutes, supporting his weight on his one good leg, and running the palms of both hands over the wall's uneven surfaces at chest level. He wasn't sure what he was hoping to find. It was more an act of animal instinct than reasoned thought. But whatever he wished to discover, it didn't materialise.

Harry sank to his knees, drowning in an ever-deepening sea of despair, and began crawling again, first one way and then the other, trudging through reeking excrement, unseeing, reaching out into the darkness until his fingers finally felt something that sent his heart leaping. Harry's mind was filled with a new-found hope born more of desperation than rational thinking. He wasn't alone! Oh, thanks be to God! There was someone propped up in the far right-hand corner of the space, someone clothed but cold. Someone who wasn't saying a word.

Harry called out, 'Hello! Say something, please say something. Who are you? Tell me your name.' But there was no reply. Harry gripped what felt like a man's arm and shook it, gently at first, and then with greater force when silence prevailed. 'Come on, wake up, please wake up, say something. My name's Harry, I'm here with you.

We can help each other. We can escape together. You're not on your own any more.'

Harry continued speaking for what felt like an age, reluctant to accept the apparent reality. He told himself that his new-found companion was merely unconscious or deep in exhausted sleep, that he wasn't alone in that dank version of hell on earth. But deep down, he already knew the truth. The body fell to one side as Harry shook it for one final time, stiff limbs unmovable, rigid and cold. Harry reached across and touched the face, and then gripped the hair, recoiling in horror as a clump came away in his hand. He retreated urgently, reversing on all fours, withdrawing into the blackness and away from the slowly decomposing corpse.

What was it the master had said? The memories flooded back, unwelcome pictures and sounds playing behind his eyes as if in real time. The master was standing there looking down on River's battered body, a white umbrella held high above his head. Oh, *God, no, the hole, the hole!* That was it, that was definitely it. It was River. It had to be River lying there, stiff, cold and rotting. And now he was in that same dark hole, alone. River hadn't found redemption, not in this life. Maybe death had been a welcome release in the end. Maybe God had forgiven him in his suffering. Perhaps now he'd found his own version of heaven.

Harry began clawing at the nearest wall, attempting to climb up towards the unseen hatch, despairingly seeking freedom until his nails were broken and his fingertips bled. He crumpled back onto the ground, curling up on his knees, covering his face, and then began butting the wall with his head. He raised himself up and continued the process, drawing his head back and lunging forwards, smashing his forehead against the hard surface of the oak panels time and again, until welcome concussion finally provided temporary oblivion. Harry lay bleeding, blood running from his wounds, pooling under his head and slowly congealing. He pictured his father's still familiar face as he drifted in and out of consciousness. And he heard his voice calling to him, calling somewhere in the distance. 'Hello Harry, my lovely boy. Don't despair. It's great up here. Why don't you come and join me in the afterlife? What are you waiting for? If not, now, when?'

Harry opened his haunted eyes for the briefest of moments and then closed them again, drifting near to insensibility as his father's image disappeared, blending with the blackness. 'Not now, Dad, it's not time yet. I've got to... I've got to look after Mum.' Within seconds Harry was unconscious again, the conversation at an end. He was lost to a restless sleep that would end all too soon.

16

Rosie Aldridge sat parked in the busy West Wales Police headquarters car park for almost ten minutes, before finally building up sufficient resolve to exit her small family hatchback. She locked the doors with a click of a button and strode purposefully over the shiny wet tarmacadam, avoiding the many puddles with quick dancing feet, despite tottering on three-inch heels that made her look significantly taller than she actually was.

Rosie paused on approaching the entrance, asking herself if she were doing the right thing. She almost turned and rushed back towards her car in the interests of an easy life, but her conscience got the better of her. That small, but undeniable voice in her head was there again, telling her to get it done.

Rosie pushed open the heavy glass doors and walked into reception with a look of steely determination on her lightly tanned, freckled face. She approached the reception desk, reached for the arrival button and pressed it quickly, not allowing herself time to change her mind. The sound of a loud bell rang out. Rosie tapped her navy-blue court shoe against the floor until Sandra appeared behind the smoked-grey glass screen only seconds later. The long-serving receptionist smiled in friendly greeting, and said in soft, Welsh tones, 'Hello, how can I help you?'

Rosie chewed her bottom lip, frowning hard, looking down rather than meet the receptionist's gaze, her earlier resolve draining away almost to nothing. 'I, err, I heard your Inspector Laura Kesey on the Welsh radio news a few days back, talking about the missing university student. Harry, I think his name's Harry.' She took a deep breath before continuing. 'I, err, I may be able to help.'

'What's your name, please?'

'It's Rosie, Rosie Aldridge.'

Sandra pointed towards a row of four brushed aluminium seats secured to the wall opposite the reception desk. 'If you could take a seat, Ms Aldridge, I'll find out if DI Kesey's available.'

Rosie sat as instructed, crossing and uncrossing her legs, repeatedly adjusting her position as her bony buttocks pressed against the metal. She took out her phone and began flicking through family photos, anything to distract herself, anything to pass the time, until about five minutes later when a smartly dressed woman in a purple business suit appeared from the lift and approached her.

'Rosie Aldridge?'

Rosie dropped her phone into her pale-yellow handbag and stood, glad to change position. 'Yes, guilty as charged.'

Kesey shook her hand and smiled. 'I'm Detective Inspector Kesey, Laura Kesey.'

'Ah, yes, I recognise your voice.'

'The radio?'

'Yeah, I was listening in the car. It was a bit of luck, really. I could easily have missed you.'

'Sandra tells me you may be able to help with the Gilmore case. Was she correct?'

'Yes, I hope so.'

'And you didn't think of coming in before now?'

Rosie looked away. 'Yeah, sorry about that, I know it's been a few days. To be honest, I nearly didn't come at all.'

Kesey decided to let it go. 'Is it okay if I call you by your first name?'

Rosie nodded.

'Okay, Rosie, if you follow me, we'll find a free interview room where we can speak privately. How does that sound?'

'Thank you, inspector, this is all way out of my comfort zone.'

Kesey led the way, speaking without looking back. 'You can call me Laura. There's no need for formality. You're here as a witness, not a suspect.'

Rosie relaxed slightly, telling herself she was doing the right thing. That she had no real choice but to assist if she could. That it was her duty to help, whatever the inconvenience, whatever the possible disruption to her life. 'Everything I tell you will be confidential, won't it?'

Kesey glanced through a small glass pane before opening the door to interview room two, holding it wide for her witness to enter. 'Let's take this one step at a time, Rosie. Take a seat and tell me why you think you can help. Any information you can share pertinent to the case will be greatly appreciated.'

Rosie sat behind a small rectangular table, with Kesey opposite her. 'But it will be confidential, yes? People won't find out what I've told you? I want to help, really I do, but my anonymity really matters to me. If *he* finds out I've been here, there may be repercussions. I don't know what he's capable of. But if he's got the bastards abducting people off the streets now, well, things must be getting worse. My health isn't great as it is. I want no part of it.'

'You said "he". Who are you talking about exactly?'

'I need your assurance first. Without that, I'm out of here.'

'The source of any information you provide won't be shared publicly without your consent.'

'Is that a promise?'

Kesey agreed with a subtle nod of her head. 'You've got absolutely nothing to worry about. Now, I need you to tell me everything you know. Let's start with the *he* you referred to. You're obviously intimidated by the man. I need to know his name.'

Rosie swallowed hard, her shoulders pushed forward, eyes ablaze. 'He calls himself *the master*.'

'The master?'

Rosie laughed despite herself. 'Yeah, I know it sounds like something out of a sci-fi movie, but believe me, he's all too real.'

Kesey was beginning to question her witness's sanity. 'And you think this master person may have something to do with Harry Gilmore's disappearance?'

Rosie moved to the very edge of her seat. 'Oh, yes, I'm certain of it. It all fits, everything you said on the radio. The white van, the big guy in the white clothes, the attractive girls, also dressed in white. That's a lot like what happened with my sister. It's how they suck people in.'

Kesey took a notepad and pen from a cluttered drawer below the table. 'Are we still talking about the master?'

Rosie lowered her head. 'No, no, I'm talking about his followers. I don't think he'd ever get his hands dirty. He's too clever for that. I doubt he takes any risks at all. Why would he? He's got people to do that for him.'

'But he's the leader, he's the man in charge?'

'Yeah, he is, very much so.'

'Can you give me a name?'

'No, I've never known it. Just, the master, that's all my sister said.'

Kesey's disappointment was palpable. 'Can you describe him for me?'

'I've never met him.'

Kesey pushed a sheet of A4 and a biro across the table. 'If this is going to make any sense to me at all, you'll need to start at the beginning. Put your full name and contact details on there for me, and then tell me everything you know. Don't leave anything out. I'll decide if it's relevant. How does that sound?'

Rosie wrote her name, address, and telephone number. 'How long have you got? It's a complex tale.'

Kesey accepted the sheet of paper. 'Take your time. There's no rush. I've got as long as it takes.'

'It all started when Diane was eighteen.'

'Diane?'

'I'm referring to my sister, Diane Aldridge.'

'Okay, I understand. You said it started when she was eighteen, how old is she now?'

'She's a month past her twenty-first birthday.'

'And you say my radio description of Harry Gilmore's potential abduction rang true?'

'Yes, that's right. My sister joined what she liked to call "the community" after meeting a young couple dressed entirely in white in the local park. Everything changed from that day. Diane was vulnerable, just like the lad you're looking for. She wasn't abducted, but she was brainwashed, I'm sure of that. She told me she was planning to give up her job at the golf club, hand over all her savings, and move to live with a group of like-minded people in a commune somewhere in Carmarthenshire. I tried to persuade her it wasn't a good idea. But nothing I said made even the slightest difference. She was going, and that was it. They collected her the very next day, bank card and all.'

Kesey tilted her head to one side. 'You said that the commune is in Carmarthenshire. Can you be more specific?'

'I spent months looking for her without success, but then a local dairy farmer in the Llandeilo area pointed me in the direction of a religious community living deep in the remote countryside about twenty minutes' drive from the town. It seems most people in the area know it's there somewhere. They see the same white-clad members about the town from time to time. But they don't know exactly where they're based.'

'Did you find the place?'

A single tear ran down Rosie's face, settling on her collar. 'Yes, I did, in the end, despite it being remote, and well hidden in thick woodland, well off the beaten track. And I found Diane too, for all the good it did me. She agreed to see me that once with the permission of the master, but only for about ten minutes in a room fitted with cameras.'

'Cameras?'

'Yes, they were filming everything.'

'Strange.'

Rosie nodded her agreement. 'Yeah, strange doesn't begin to describe it. Diane wasn't the girl I'd known. They were her family now. She actually said that. To my face. As if I was a total stranger. Nothing I could say would change her mind. She said the master's word was law. That he was the new Messiah, the most important person in her life by far. I got the distinct impression that she couldn't get rid of me quickly enough.'

Kesey made some scribbled notes, using her own form of short hand to speed the process. 'Where's Diane now?'

'She's still there, as far as I know. I did call at the compound one more time a couple of months after my first visit, but I wasn't allowed in. A man at the gate told me she'd refused to see me. That it was her right to choose. I tried to argue the point, saying I wanted to hear it from Diane's own mouth, but he became abusive. Not physically, I'm not saying he hit me or anything awful like that. But I was intimidated. He called me worthless, unworthy of my sister's love. I still dream about it sometimes, nightmares, it really shook me up.'

'Are you saying you haven't seen or spoken to your sister since that first visit, not even by phone?'

'Yes, that's exactly what I'm saying. I'd call it a cult rather than a community. Those people stole my sister. They took her from my family and me. They didn't actually abduct her, not in any physical sense, but they may as well have. They twisted her mind. It's my mother I feel most sorry for. Diane broke her heart. I'll never forgive her for that.'

'What was your impression of the commune, that first time when you were allowed in? What did you think of the place?'

Rosie wrung her hands together, thinking back to that time, picturing events in her mind. 'There was a tension about the entire community. As if something bad were about to happen at any second. People were all dressed the same, white trousers, white tops, and they were walking about like zombies.'

Kesey's eyebrows arched. 'Zombies? What do you mean, exactly?'

'It's hard to explain, really. You'd know what I mean if you'd been there.'

'Please give it a try. Anything you tell me could be helpful.'

'Everyone I saw seemed expressionless, you know, blank-faced, avoiding my eyes as if they were hiding something. And that included my sister. I'd never seen her like that before. It was like her personality had been sucked out of her. She just kept repeating the same things. She wanted to stay. It was time for me to leave. And then she started chanting. Actually chanting! "God is great. I am nothing. All praise to the master." She was yelling it as I left the room and made my way towards the exit in a flood of tears. "All praise to the master. All praise to the master." She just didn't shut up. I actually thought she may have gone insane. I don't know, maybe she had.'

Kesey bounced a knee. 'Nothing you've said constitutes a crime. It's concerning, yes, but criminal, no. There's nothing that could result in prosecution.'

'Okay, I'm sorry, I hope I haven't wasted your time.'

Kesey rose to her feet, smiling. 'No, you haven't, not for a minute. Are you familiar with Google Maps?'

'Yes, I've used it once or twice over the years. Why do you ask?'

'If I get a tablet, could you show me where the compound is?'

'Um, yeah, I don't see why not. It's not going to be marked on any map, that's for sure. But I can show you the general area.'

Kesey was beginning to think she'd hit lucky. Sometimes a break was all you needed. 'I'll be back with you in two minutes. I'm sorry you didn't come to see me sooner, but I'm glad you came. I am going to find out exactly what's going on in that place if it's the last thing I do. Your information is very welcome. I really do appreciate your help.'

17

Harry covered his eyes, blinded by the light of the sun, as Baptist opened the metal hatch and looked down at him at six o'clock that morning.

The big man shouted, 'How are you doing down there, newbie? Have you prayed to God? Have you begged forgiveness for your sins? We're approaching the end times. The signs are everywhere. Humanity's running out of time. And so are you, my brother. You need to seek redemption before it's too late.'

Harry peered towards the light. 'Water, please, I need w-water.'

Baptist picked up a full bucket from the ground and hurled it over Harry, soaking his entire body. 'There you go. Aren't you lucky I brought some with me. Lap it up, newbie. It's the only water you'll get today. There's no more after that. You don't deserve a cup. Not after what you've done. Your sins are far too wicked for that.'

Harry lowered his hand as his eyes gradually adjusted to the brightness. He lapped at a small pool of water settled in the earth and then pointed to the slowly decomposing corpse lying in one corner a few feet away, surrounded by insects. 'Look, there's a, there's a b-body in here w-with me. It's River, he's, he's, he's dead. You can't, you can't leave me in here with that, not with that!'

'It's God's will. It's the master's will. Do you think you know better?'

'I didn't say that, I didn't...'

The big man tossed a green apple into the pit and laughed. 'Are you lost for words, newbie? Oh, dear, such a sad sight to behold. I understand your concerns, really I do. But River's death was just. It was no more than he deserved. His demise proves his guilt. No doubt, his spirit will burn in hell for all of eternity. Let his presence be a reminder to you. Wrestle with your conscience. River has failed his test. Now it's your turn to determine your fate. Pray, newbie, pray. No one can do it for you.'

Harry flung his arms up. 'He just tried to l-leave the compound, that's all, he only tried to leave! Is that so t-terrible? There must be worse sins. Surely, he didn't deserve to die.' He pointed at the body. 'Not here, not like that!'

Baptist cracked his knuckles. 'Are you questioning the master's true wisdom, newbie? Do you really think that's sensible? Because that's what got you in there in the first place. Do you remember? Two nights ago, when you insulted his name. You need to repent and atone. You're going to end up dead and tortured by the devil's demons in the darkest corner of hell, if you're not very careful. It's reserved for the disloyal.' He pointed to River, a look of disgust on his face. 'People like that piece of shit who lack faith and let the community down. Forget about River, it's too late for him. Maybe you've still got a chance of redemption. Concentrate on saving yourself.'

Harry scuttled through the thick mud on all fours and picked up the apple. He looked at it for a few seconds before taking a bite, chewing, and swallowing. 'I understand what you're s-saying. I get it, really, I do. I've prayed, I've repented for hour after hour when alone in the dark. Let me out of here, *please*, I'm b-begging you. I am so very sorry. I can't stand it in here for another second. I'll do better. I p-promise, I'll do better.'

Baptist gripped the heavy metal hatch, holding it upright, keeping it half open. 'What happened to your head?'

'I, err, I banged it when I fell.'

Baptist lowered the hatch an inch or two, reducing the light. 'Oh, I don't think so, newbie. I saw you fall. I dropped you. You hit the earth feet first. Those injuries are self-inflicted. And that's the devil's work. You tried to escape your punishment. You compounded one sin with another. You are far from redemption. Leaving you in there is an act of kindness. Allowing you to leave prematurely would be the worst thing I could ever do. The master taught me that. His wisdom is beyond comparison.'

Harry placed his hands together as if in prayer. 'Please d-don't lock me in again, not in the dark, not with that stinking corpse. I can't stand it, Baptist. Please, I'll do anything, anything!'

The big man sighed. 'God is testing you, my brother. Think of it as a privilege, an opportunity to grow spiritually. Had River done so, had he embraced the chance he was given, he'd still be breathing now, instead of lying in the rancid dirt with you, a meal for the worms. Don't make the same mistake. The master has ruled that you must spend seven days in the ground. Two have already passed. There's just five to go. I suggest you use that time wisely. If you survive, it will be God's will. You'll be forgiven. All will be well. You'll be a much-loved member of the community once more. But if you fail again, you die. It's natural justice in its most perfect form. God is great. All praise to the master.'

'Five more days! Five fucking days! No, please, I can't s-stand it, kill me, kill me now! I'd rather die than spend another moment in this hellhole. I'm begging you, Baptist. Get me out of here or put an end to it now. I'm ready to meet my maker.'

Baptist scratched his beard, stretched, and yawned loudly, the bellowing sound echoing in the trees before fading away to silence. 'Your words offend me. Have you learned nothing in your time in the ground? Whether you survive or not depends on God's will. It's a matter for Him and only Him. Your life is not your own. Soon you will return to darkness. You'll be secure in the womb of the earth with life and death all around you. You'll either come out a new creation, your sins forgiven, or you'll join River in hell. It depends on the strength of your faith. Pray, newbie, pray! It really is up to you.'

Harry let out a guttural scream that sent the birds flying. 'Then, get River's c-corpse out of here. It's rotting, maggot-infested. Look at it, the entire enclosure is putrid. I can't stop gagging. Will you at least do that for me? Surely, that's not too much to ask, is it? It's the godly thing to do.'

'Do you speak for God?'

'No, no, I wasn't, I wasn't...' Harry collapsed to the earth and wept.

Baptist walked away, returning about ten minutes later with a shovel in hand. He tossed it into the semi-darkness of the hole, missing Harry by inches. 'Bury the transgressor approximately two feet under the earth, that's the optimum depth for decomposition. Anything less is unacceptable. And dig a suitably sized hole for your own shit, you're a man, not an animal. I want this place looking a lot more presentable when I return tomorrow. I find the stench offensive.'

Harry called out as Baptist closed the hatch tight shut, returning the hole to darkness. 'How the fuck do I dig without light? And my leg! I think my leg's broken. I can't stand without falling over. How do I dig a fucking hole?'

Baptist shook his head knowingly. He secured the hatch without another word, sliding the stiff, large metal bolt across, and placing the two heavy grassy pallets back in place. As he strolled back in the direction of the compound, humming, it was as if Harry had never existed. There was just a field of green grass surrounded by trees and nothing more to see. Harry screamed and continued screaming until he collapsed, hoarse and exhausted. But nobody heard him. The muffled, barely audible sound of his desperate, anguished suffering was lost in the cold earth. Baptist looked back and smiled at one point, as he pictured Harry in that place, searching for absolution. The master was such a clever man, a genius. That's what Baptist believed with every cell of his being, with no room for doubt. Where would they all be without their esteemed leader to guide them towards the light? *Praise be to the master, praise be!* He was a father to them all. Everything was exactly as it should be. Shadow was in the ground. All was right with the world. No pain no gain. The master's plan had worked out perfectly.

18

DI Kesey, DC Peter Best, better known as George, and two uniformed female officers with search training, sat in the force's shiny, black, four-wheel drive SUV, with Best in the driver's seat. Kesey had determined the best route to the isolated rural compound, and she'd decided that an unannounced early morning visit would be to their best advantage. An element of surprise was almost always a good thing, particularly where a search was concerned.

She'd experienced some initial difficulty convincing a local magistrate of the need for a warrant the previous evening. But Kesey's notoriously effective persuasive skills had eventually triumphed, and she now had the essential piece of paper, signed and folded in the inside pocket of her olive-green, summer-weight linen jacket.

Kesey was feeling both tired and slightly jaded following a disturbed night, caused by her son's frustratingly virulent, bacterial respiratory illness, which had dragged on for almost two weeks without any significant signs of improvement. But she was determined to make the most of the day, however exhausted, however concerned she felt. Home was home, and work was work. She had to remain professional. One couldn't affect the other. It was something she'd learned early in her career, something her old DI had stressed, and she'd stuck to it ever since.

If Harry Gilmore was anywhere in the remote, quasi-religious community she'd been told so much about, she planned to find him.

Best drove away from the police headquarters car park at just after 5am, steering left into the quiet road, and heading east along the A40 in the direction of Llandeilo, via the verdant, bright and striking River Tywi Valley. Within half an hour they'd passed through the small historic town, and were negotiating a narrow single-track road deep into the west Wales countryside with high hedgerows to either side. When Kesey spotted a sharp right-hand turning onto a stone-strewn track leading up towards a large area of dense woodland, she felt sure they'd found the correct place. This was it. They were almost there. It was time to stop chatting. Time to get into work mode and focus. She was in charge, the boss. It was time to take control.

Best signalled to his right, more out of habit than anything else. 'Do you think this is it, ma'am?'

Kesey looked down at her smartphone and frowned. 'My internet signal packed in about fifteen minutes ago, but, yeah, I reckon so. I'd say the compound is somewhere up there in the middle of those trees at the top of the hill. You could hide a small village in that lot without too much trouble.'

Best lifted his foot from the accelerator pedal, slowing almost to a stop and turning his head towards his boss. 'So, do you want me to keep going?'

'Yeah, but take it easy, and keep the revs low. We don't want to give them any clues we're on the way unless we have to.'

'Okay, will do.'

Within ten minutes Best was driving deep into a dense woodland bathed in only limited light, due to the expansive leafy canopy. He continued the journey, negotiating one sharp bend after another until a pair of high wooden gates topped with razor wire came into view to their left. Best brought the SUV to a halt, applied the handbrake and stared incredulously, along with the others. 'Look at the size of the fucking place! How the fuck they got planning permission for that lot is a complete mystery to me.'

Kesey nodded. 'Maybe they haven't got permission. I read something about temporary structures. The rules are different. Or maybe no one from the council has ever been here.'

Best unfastened his seat belt. 'Might be worth checking out.'

'Yeah, maybe, but let's focus on trying to find Harry Gilmore for now. That's our number one priority. Anything else is a distraction.'

Best suddenly said what he'd been thinking for some time. 'Even if Gilmore is here, it doesn't mean that they kidnapped the bloke. That girl he was with was something of a looker. I wouldn't say no. He may want to be here. There may not have been a crime at all.'

Kesey glared at him. 'I don't think so.'

'Oh, come on, Laura, you have to admit it's a possibility.'

'It's ma'am or boss to you. Gilmore's disappearance has been well publicised – TV, radio, local papers. If he's here of his own free will, why hasn't someone told us about it? You saw the tape as well as I did. I told the chief super, and I'm telling you, it looks like an abduction to me.'

'Yeah, but it's not obvious, that's all I'm saying. It's not like the CPS are going to look at it and agree to a prosecution anytime soon. If it is an abduction, we need more evidence before making arrests. There's no point in pulling someone in and then letting them go again. That would achieve fuck all.'

Kesey gritted her teeth. 'I'm very well aware of that, thank you, Peter.'

'I was just thinking out loud, that's all.'

'Well, don't, there's a time and place, and this isn't it. Concentrate on what you're here to do. We find Gilmore, we talk to him, and then I'll decide on the next step. Got it?'

'Yes, ma'am, loud and clear.'

Kesey swivelled in her seat. 'Are you two okay in the back, you're both ready, you know what you're here for?'

Both women nodded, suddenly on full alert, keen to get on with the job.

Kesey opened her front passenger door, followed by the others, who exited the vehicle and walked behind her in the direction of the high gates. Best's unsuccessful efforts to open them were met with the sound of a security camera pivoting on top of a tall metal post to their immediate right, pointing in their direction and obviously focussed on them. When Kesey held up her plastic laminated warrant card in clear view, pointing it towards the camera lens and shouting, 'Police', a crackling speaker erupted into sound.

A male voice intended to exude assertive authority blared out for all to hear. 'This is private property. You are trespassing. We are a law-abiding religious community with charity status. Please get back in your vehicle and return to wherever you came from. Your intrusion is both unwelcome and unjustified.'

Kesey took the search warrant from her pocket as Best shook the gates to little effect. She looked up at the camera and yelled, 'It's the police. We've got a warrant to search this place. Open up!'

'Our community lives by God's law. We do not recognise your rules. I've asked you to leave. Please comply.'

Kesey's tone deepened. 'You can open up and let us in, or I'll contact whoever I need to, to break the gates down. Either way, we're searching the place today. Make your choice. You've got five minutes to make a decision. After that, I'm calling in the bulldozers.'

All was silent for a few seconds before the tannoy system crackled back into life. There was a subtle tremor in the man's voice when he spoke again. 'Please give me sufficient time to consult the master. Only he can decide on the appropriate course of action. His word is law here.'

Kesey tapped her watch. 'I'll give you another five minutes in the interests of co-operation. But no more, not a second longer, and that is not negotiable.'

'I'll return as quickly as I can.'

Nicola, the older of the two uniformed policewomen, turned to Kesey after about two minutes had passed. 'What are we going to do if they don't open up, boss?'

Kesey gave a short laugh. 'Fuck knows. We lost any element of surprise long ago. I'm going to continue bluffing and keep my fingers crossed. If that doesn't work, your guess is as good as mine. I'll have to take advice from the top brass. We didn't have many wood and wire compounds in Birmingham.'

The four officers had almost given up on searching the compound that morning when one of the two gates suddenly began to move outwards, pushed by a huge, well-muscled man dressed entirely in white, who ran a hand through his long hair and introduced himself as Baptist.

'You can come in on sufferance. But please respect the sanctity of our loving community. Our glorious master is to grant you an audience. I will take you to him now. He is waiting for you. I hope you appreciate how much of an honour that is. Not everyone is as fortunate.'

Both Kesey and Best recognised Baptist as the driver, the man who'd lifted Harry into the van, the man caught on CCTV, but they didn't say anything. It was far too soon for that.

Baptist ushered the officers through the open gate and into the compound with a beckoning wave of his hand. 'If you follow me, our leader is waiting for you. You can explain the reason for your visit to him. He's an important man. I hope you don't waste too much of his time.'

Kesey chose not to respond. There would be plenty of time for talking. She walked alongside the big man, leading her three officers through the grounds of the community and towards the parade ground, where to their astonishment, a white-robed, somewhat overweight, otherwise unremarkable middle-aged man, was sitting on what looked like a golden throne with his hands resting on his knees. Kesey felt inclined to laugh when she first saw him. The sight was just so unexpected. So out of place in the Welsh countryside. But she somehow managed to suppress her instinct, as did the others, following her lead. Cameron was the first to speak. 'Welcome to our small community. What can I do for you fine officers? We're always happy to help if we can.'

Kesey approached him. 'Let's start with introductions. My name is Detective Inspector Laura Kesey, West Wales Police. And you are?'

'My followers call me the master.'

Kesey shook her head with a sneer she couldn't suppress, however hard she tried. 'No, your name, your legal name, the name on your birth certificate.'

'I was known as Vincent Cameron before God chose me to lead my followers to paradise.'

'It's good to meet you, Mr Cameron.'

Baptist tensed as Cameron rose to his feet. 'It's *Professor* Cameron, *Professor*, but I prefer the title, master. I would hope you'd show me the respect my position here demands.'

Kesey took a colour photo of Harry from her handbag, as the sky darkened, threatening rain. 'We're here looking for a nineteen-year-old university student by the name of Harry Gilmore.' She went to hand Cameron the photo but withdrew it quickly when he didn't accept it.

'I'm told you have a warrant. Is that correct?'

Kesey took the document from her pocket. 'You'll find it entitles us to search all areas we deem necessary and to seize any materials we consider relevant to our investigation.'

Cameron unfolded the piece of paper and began reading, holding it just a few inches from his face to accommodate his deteriorating eyesight, rather than use his reading glasses. 'Quite so, quite so, I can see it all here in black and white. Although I don't know what you think you're going to find. We're a law-abiding group. Thou shalt not kill, thou shalt not steal, and so on. We follow God's commandments to the letter with no exceptions. Criminality of any kind would never be tolerated.'

'If you could take a look at the photograph, Professor Cameron, that should expedite matters.'

He took it from her hand, glancing at it briefly before returning it. 'Ah, yes, young Harry, a nice lad we were pleased to welcome with love. He was here for a time, but he left very soon after his arrival. Our lifestyle wasn't for him. That's what he told me. I can't help you any more than that, I'm afraid.' He turned away from Kesey, looking towards Baptist. 'That's correct, isn't it? Did young Harry mention where he planned to go next?'

'Not to me, master.'

'Is there anything you can add to further assist these fine officers? You have my permission to tell them anything they need to know. Hold nothing back.'

The big man gathered his thoughts. 'Harry joined us after meeting Achara in a Carmarthen bar, but their relationship didn't last. He left two days after his arrival. And that's all I know. He came, and he went. It's a shame really, he seemed like a nice boy.'

Kesey looked up at the grey sky as large drops of rain began to fall. 'Is there somewhere we can speak inside?'

Cameron pointed to Baptist, and then the painted throne. 'If you follow me, inspector, we can talk in my private quarters. I'm sure you'll find them comfortable.'

Baptist rushed the throne away, as the four officers followed Cameron in the direction of a large wooden building surrounded by summer flowers. Kesey stopped at the entrance, focussing her attention on the two uniformed constables, who were standing on the porch trying to stay dry under an overhanging slate roof. 'If you two start going through the various buildings, that would be helpful. You know who you're looking for. If you see or hear anything relevant, let me know immediately. George, you stay with me for the moment. Are we all clear?'

All three nodded.

'Okay, we're here to find Harry Gilmore. Let's get it done.' Cameron lay back on his large and comfortable bed, head propped up on three plump silk-covered pillows, leaving Kesey and Best staring at him incredulously, stunned by his eccentricity. The professor wasn't like anyone they'd ever met before, despite their years of experience. And dealing with him was proving something of a challenge.

Kesey took the lead. 'Harry Gilmore was seen on CCTV being carried into a white van by the man you referred to as Baptist. Harry was clearly drunk or drugged. I believe he was brought here against his will.'

'Oh, dear, that is disappointing. I made myself perfectly clear when we were outside. I was good enough to bring you out of the rain. We're a law-abiding bunch, as I've already explained. Do I really need to repeat myself?'

Kesey had already taken a strong dislike to a man she thought ridiculous. 'You can answer our questions here, or at the police station. It's up to you.'

Cameron laughed, gaining confidence. 'Oh, I very much doubt you have a power of arrest in these particular circumstances. I am correct, aren't I, inspector? I'm sure you'll tell me if that's not the case.'

Kesey didn't reply, but her expression betrayed her irritation. Cameron chuckled to himself. 'Harry was delighted to come here, and he was free to leave whenever he chose. I've told you what happened. Baptist has confirmed it. I feel sure Achara would be happy to do likewise.'

'Achara?'

'I'm referring to the beautiful young woman Harry took such a liking to. I'm sure Baptist will have spoken to her by now. She'll be aware of your visit, as will all my other followers. Perhaps you'd like to speak to her too. I can arrange it if you like. All you have to do is ask.'

Best interjected, more annoyed by the second. 'There were two females in the vehicle at the time of Gilmore's potential abduction. Who was the second one?'

'Potential, potential, now that's an interesting choice of words. You seem far from sure there was any crime at all. I hope you're not going to waste much more of my time. I'm a busy man.'

'I asked you the name of the second female.'

'Oh, what a shame! I hope you didn't intend to interview Mary. She's away visiting friends. I don't know where, and she's not contactable. She's an old-fashioned girl. She's never owned a mobile. And I've no idea what her surname is. She didn't share it. I think she wanted to forget an unhappy past. She often said that Mary was name enough.'

There was a knock on the door before either officer had the opportunity to comment further. It was opened by Baptist, who held it open for Achara to enter. Kesey strongly suspected she was about to say exactly what she'd been told to say. It seemed obvious, as predictable as night and day.

Kesey asked the same questions and received the same answers, which was no more than she'd expected. She asked both Cameron and his two followers if they'd be prepared to make written statements. All three confirmed that they would, happily. Why wouldn't they? They had nothing to hide.

Kesey then asked Best to stay with the two men while she spoke to Achara outside on the porch. Achara protested initially, saying she had nothing more to add, but she eventually agreed when encouraged by Cameron. 'Go and talk to the nice officer with my blessing, my child. Have faith. God will protect you. You know what to say. You have nothing to fear. Let the spirit guide you.'

Kesey led Achara from the building, and a sufficient distance from the front door to ensure they weren't overheard. She spoke with passion. Keen to stress urgency. Still hopeful of gaining her interviewee's help and support. 'Harry is missing, Achara. He hasn't got access to prescribed medication that's essential to his health. His mother is fearful for his life. I'm told you're fond of him. If that's true, you'll tell me exactly what happened. If you can give me any clues as to his location, you could be saving his life. This couldn't be more important. I can't stress that enough. This is your opportunity to co-operate. No one's listening but me.'

'The master hears all.'

Kesey touched her wrist. 'He's inside the building with my officer. This is your chance to speak freely.'

'Harry wanted to come here, and then he wanted to leave. There's nothing more to say.'

'Where is he, Achara? I know you know something. I can see it in your face.'

'Harry came, and Harry went. He is no longer my concern. I

hope you find him, but he is not my responsibility. He is the captain of his own ship. He steers his own course, with God's help.'

The skin bunched around Kesey's eyes. 'You need to listen to me, and you need to listen well. If you played any part in bringing Harry here against his will, you will be prosecuted and locked up. That's unless you co-operate with me right now. Kidnapping and false imprisonment are extremely serious offences. You could be sent to prison for a very long time. I'd think about that very carefully if I were you. Help me now, or you'll be treated as a suspect along with the rest.'

Achara smiled. 'He came and then he went. God is great. All praise to the master!'

'What did you say?'

'Some of us respect our betters. You have much to learn.'

'Harry was heavily intoxicated when you led him to that van. Can you explain that for me? And don't even think about lying. Everything you did is recorded on film.'

'Harry was drunk when I met him. He'd split up from a girlfriend and was drowning his sorrows. I felt obliged to look after him. It was my duty as a child of God. I thought coming here would both cheer Harry up and help him to realise what is really important in life.'

'What's that exactly?'

Achara smiled again, radiant. 'Faith, loyalty, and hard work.'

'Where is he, Achara? I know you're lying.'

She looked at Kesey with a blank expression, bored. 'Can I go now? I have tasks to complete. Work purifies the soul.'

'Just answer the question.'

'Harry came, and then he went. If you ask me the same question a thousand times, I'll give you the same answer. I've told you the truth and nothing but the truth. Isn't that the legal term? I can't do any more than that.'

Kesey lowered her tone, speaking in a whisper. 'If you're scared, I can protect you. I'm here with three other officers. You can leave with us when we go. I'll guarantee your safety.'

Achara shook her head and grinned. 'You really are in need of enlightenment. I have nothing to fear. But, you, on the other hand, will face God's wrath for interfering in the master's work. Leave now, or God will curse you and yours for all of eternity. You have no idea of the dangers you face.'

'Who are you scared of, Achara? Is it the man you call master, or Baptist? Or maybe it's both of them. I'm guessing it's both of them.'

'Am I under arrest?'

Kesey shook her head. 'No, you're not. Yet.'

Achara turned and walked away without another word. Kesey called after her, but all Achara did was wave. As she picked up her pace, Achara shouted out, 'Harry came, and Harry went. His disappearance is God's will. God is great. All praise to the master. Did you hear me, inspector? All praise to the master!'

Kesey gathered her officers together in a corner of the water-soaked parade ground about an hour later, shortly after the rain stopped falling. None of them had found anything significant. And none had heard anything of interest either, other than the fact that the children were home-schooled. Any white-clad member of the community they'd encountered simply said they knew nothing of Harry's whereabouts. Best had obtained Cameron and Baptist's full names and dates of birth for checking against the police crime intelligence system, but that was as good as it got. Best had wandered into the field beyond the vegetable gardens at one point, but all he found was a plastic bucket on top of a couple of pallets with grass growing through them. And that, Best decided, wasn't worth another thought. It was just a bucket. Where was the significance in that?

19

Baptist knocked on Cameron's office door and waited to be asked in for almost five minutes before finally receiving a response.

'Come!'

Baptist opened the door slowly, peeping in, weighing up his master's mood before entering. 'The pigs have finally gone, master. Praise be! I watched them drive off. God saved us. They looked, but they didn't find a thing.'

Cameron turned to face him, swivelling in his office chair and looking up, a distorted expression of rage transforming his features. 'The police came here, Baptist! They actually entered our private sanctuary. They stuck their noses in where they don't belong. How dare they?' He was on his feet now, shouting, angrier than ever before. 'Who do they think they are? How dare they interfere in God's holy work!'

Baptist mumbled his words. 'They didn't find anything, master. It's a triumph for all of us. And something tells me they won't be back.'

Cameron hurled a pottery mug across the room. It hit a wall, and smashed into jagged pieces. 'Oh, I know they won't be back, Baptist. I know they won't come back because I'm going to make sure they don't come back. God has told me to punish the two detectives for their impudence. Did you hear me, Baptist? God has told me that the interfering swine deserve to die a horrible death.'

Baptist dropped to his knees, linking his hands together in front of him. 'What, both of them, master? Are they to have no opportunity for redemption? Doesn't everyone deserve the chance to confess, however terrible their sins?'

'Are you questioning my wisdom? Are you succumbing to the devil's influence? I need you to stay strong, man! Now is not the time for weakness. God's work is far too important for that.'

Baptist kissed Cameron's bare foot. 'I can only apologise, master. Please forgive me. If you want me to kill them, I'm happy to do God's work. Tell me what to do, and I'll do it.'

Cameron was calmer now, pacing the room, hands linked behind him, pondering his reply. 'I'll pray, I'll talk to God, and then I'll decide who will serve as His honoured executioners. Perhaps we should let Kesey live awhile after all. Perhaps we should bring her here to experience real suffering. We could string her up for all my children to witness. Or put her in the hole and leave her there to starve. Or crucify her, yes, yes, we could crucify her! There's a poetic beauty to it, a natural justice. Why didn't I think of it before? Crucifixion would be our exalted community's greatest triumph! A sacrifice, yes, a sacrifice, that will signal God's final blessing for his chosen children. The end times are fast approaching, Baptist. Kesey's death will signal the end of this world and the beginning of the next! Today was meant to happen. The pigs were meant to visit. Nothing else makes sense. God sent them here as a sacrifice to save us from our sins.'

Baptist jumped to his feet, leaping one way and then another, throwing his arms up, shouting out his praise as Cameron looked on, clapping. 'Yes, yes! God is great. All praise to the master. I am nothing. Thank you, master. The pigs have to die!'

20

Janet handed Kesey a yellow mug filled almost to the brim with freshly ground Puerto Rican coffee, and smiled. 'There you go, Ed's finally asleep. Time to relax.'

'Thanks, love, you're a star. I was beginning to think he'd never settle down.'

Janet sat next to Kesey on the three-seater settee, squeezing up close. 'I think I know that book of his word for word by now. He always wants the same frigging one. I'd like to kick that caterpillar right in the arse.'

Kesey laughed. 'It'll be my turn to read to him tomorrow night. I should be home in time.'

'Do you fancy a film?'

'Yeah, why not? You choose.'

'Not a chance, you're fussier than me.'

Kesey picked up the remote, flicked through the channels, stopped, and then started again. 'Something tells me we've had this conversation before.'

'What's up, Laura? I know there's something. I haven't seen you this tense for ages. You're not still worrying about Edward, are you?'

Kesey sipped her coffee. 'No, I know he's on the mend.'

'What is it then?'

'Oh, it's just this case I'm dealing with.'

'Which one?'

'Do you really want to know?'

'I asked, didn't I?'

'Okay, it's this business with the missing student. The one I talked about on the radio. I know the mother socially. The boy suffers from depression, and it's up to me to find him alive. I've got to admit the pressure's getting to me.'

Janet gripped Kesey's free hand, holding it tight with affection. 'That doesn't sound like you. You can usually cope with almost anything.'

'Yeah, I know, but the mum teaches my yoga class. This one feels personal.'

'Are you not making any progress at all?'

Kesey shook her head. 'No, I really don't think we are. I'm sure those religious nutters have still got him hidden somewhere. But I can't find him, and I've got nothing to prove anything. All I've got is a couple of minor offences that are hardly worth bothering with. I feel as if they're running rings around me.'

'Calling them nutters is a bit strong, isn't it?'

'You wouldn't say that if you'd met them for yourself.'

'What's that supposed to mean?'

'They were all dressed in white. The men, the women, the kids, every single one of them. And they all seem to worship a screwball who calls himself the master. He's an ex-university lecturer who claims to perform miracles. I checked him out online. He makes a lot of bold claims, a lot of his followers are discussing things he's supposed to have done, but there's no real evidence of any of it actually happening. I'm convinced he's a con man and a dangerous one too. Weird doesn't begin to describe it.'

Janet placed her mug back on the glass-topped coffee table. 'You said white, yes?'

'You know I did.'

'There was a woman dressed in white standing outside the house this afternoon.'

Kesey's hand flew to her chest. 'Doing what?'

'She was just standing there on the pavement on the opposite side of the road, looking at the house.'

Kesey crossed the room to open the curtains. 'She's not there now. Can you describe her for me?'

'What is it, Laura? Do I need to be worried?'

Kesey paused, considering her choice of words. 'I'm not sure, to be honest. I think I may have seen a van driven by one of the followers a few cars behind me on my way home from work yesterday. The bastards could be following me.'

Janet took a blue plastic asthma inhaler from a trouser pocket, administering an urgent puff. 'But you can't be sure?'

'No, not really. Whoever it was turned off before I had the chance to check them out.'

'Oh, God, not again, Laura, not after all the shit we went through with the Newman case. That maniac nearly killed you, and now this. I can't bear it, not with a child in the house. I've told you to leave the job. I've told you police work isn't conducive to happy family life. What if one of us gets hurt? It's time for you to listen to me for once. Surely there must be other jobs you could do to pay the bills.'

Kesey tried to hug her partner but gave up on the idea when Janet pulled away. 'I shouldn't have said anything at all. It's almost certainly something and nothing. They're probably just trying to rattle me. Or maybe the vehicle I saw wasn't anything to do with them at all. We could be worrying about nothing.'

A vein pulsed on Janet's neck, her blood pressure leaping. 'But what if we're not, Laura? What if we're not? Newman nearly killed you, and now you've got some other nutters after you. When's it ever going to end? Is any job worth all that?'

'I'll get it sorted. I'll pay them another visit. I'll have a word with the man in charge and warn him off.'

The contours of Janet's face relaxed slightly. 'Do you really think that'll work?'

When Kesey replied, 'Yes,' a few brief moments later, she sounded a lot more confident than she felt.

'She was Asian, young and beautiful. The girl watching the house, that's what she looked like, the girl in white.'

Kesey turned away. 'Okay, leave it with me. I'll sort it. I know exactly who it was. This will all be over before you know it. You can trust me on that.'

'I hope so, Laura. I really hope so. This isn't the sort of life I want to live. I don't know how much more I can take.'

21

Baptist removed the two grassy pallets, slid back the bolt, opened the heavy metal hatch, looked down, and smiled. 'Your seven days are up, newbie. It's good news. Today's the day you're out of there. Praise be to God! Your sins are forgiven.'

Harry lay hunched, retreating inwardly, in a dank corner next to River's recently dug grave.

Baptist aimed a small stone at Harry's head, bouncing it off a shoulder. 'Didn't you hear me, newbie? You've survived. I can see you breathing. God has spared you.'

Harry tried to stand, allowing the wall to support his weight, but his legs collapsed under him. He lay on the damp earth, weeping.

Baptist threw down a rope, wrapping the other end around one of his powerful arms. 'I need you to tie that around your waist for me, newbie. Do you think you can do that one thing? Come on, move! If you want out of there, you've got to help.'

But Harry didn't move. He'd faded into semi-consciousness, born of the need for nourishment. He looked thinner and he looked weaker. Every breath was laboured, shallow. He was barely clinging onto life.

Baptist threw a larger stone, aiming carefully, finding his target this time. 'Come on, newbie. Wake up and smell the coffee. Give thanks to God. Give thanks to the master. Come out of the ground. He has an important task for you to perform.'

Harry forced his eyes open, his dark world slowly coming back into focus. 'Water, please, I need w-water.'

'If you look to your right, you'll find a rope. I need you to tie the damned thing around your waist. There will be plenty of time to drink when you're out of there. You need to be patient. Patience is a virtue. Ask God for strength.'

Harry climbed onto his knees, wincing in pain with each movement. His white clothing was stained, unrecognisable as the garments he'd donned a week before.

'Do not make me come down there, newbie. That wouldn't be a good idea. It wouldn't be a good idea at all.'

Harry used all the strength he could muster to wrap the rope around his emaciated waist while asking himself why it felt so very heavy. He tied a double knot, close to total exhaustion but driven by the desire to be free. Harry looked up at Baptist, screwing up his eyes against the light, pupils reduced to pinpoints. 'That's it, it's, it's, done. Please, p-please get me out of here.' A part of him feared it was a bluff. That he'd be left there to die, despite the big man's promises. And his relief was overwhelming, sending him into a spiral of wild emotion when he felt the rope tighten around his body. 'Thank you, Baptist. I'm so, so, v-very grateful.'

The big man pulled, walking slowly backwards, dragging Harry up the side of his underground cell a few agonising inches at a time. When Harry finally scrambled out onto the grass minutes later, his gratitude was gushing. He thanked God, he thanked the master, and he thanked Baptist as his saviour.

Baptist untied the rope, clutched Harry by his right wrist, and began dragging him across the field, choosing not to lift him as before for risk of spoiling his own clothes. 'Chant along with me, Shadow. Shout out your praise. God is great. I am nothing. All praise to the master. Come on, you can do it. Wake up, man! God will give you strength. Chant, Shadow, chant!'

Harry struggled to join in with Baptist's rallying call, crying out the mantra in barely audible tones, his voice faltering as he gulped the air. Harry kept chanting increasingly incoherently for almost five minutes more until exhaustion finally took over and silenced him. The big man glanced back at Harry and grinned on approaching the dormitory. Shadow had survived the hole, but that was only a beginning. If he thought his trials were over, he was very sadly mistaken. *God is great. All praise to the master!* There were bigger challenges to come.

22

'Can I have a word, ma'am?'

Kesey looked up from her double egg and chips, checking the clock on the canteen wall. 'Make it quick, George. I've got a bowl of rhubarb crumble and custard with my name on it.'

Best sat opposite his boss, a cup of freshly brewed tea in one hand and a bacon roll in the other. 'I've had Achara on the phone, the British Asian girl. She wants to meet up somewhere and talk on a one-to-one, anywhere but the station.'

Kesey sat upright in her seat. 'Did she tell you what it's all about?'

'She's escaped the cult and needs help.'

Kesey chewed and swallowed. 'Well, I guess it sounds hopeful. Set up a meeting. She may know where Gilmore is. What have we got to lose?'

* * *

Achara spotted Peter Best sitting, cross-legged and reading a tabloid newspaper, on a public bench in a quiet corner of

Carmarthen Park, at shortly after 3 p.m. that same afternoon. She approached him slowly, coming up from behind, and whispering, 'Hello', directly into his ear.

Best turned to look at her, red-faced and smiling. Seconds later, she cut his throat from ear to ear. Achara thrust the point of the razor-sharp blade deep into the side of Best's neck, dragging it sideways, slicing through flesh and sinew with surprising ease, until the edge connected with bone. Best slumped off the bench, dark blood pouring in full satanic flow from his twitching body as he hit the ground.

Achara strolled away, clutching the knife tightly in one hand, and singing a soaring hymn of praise as if nothing of any significance had happened at all. She began skipping along as she left the park and finally burst into a trot as she continued her journey through the outskirts of the town in the direction of West Wales Police headquarters.

Achara was heavily stained with Best's congealed blood, but sweating only slightly, when she handed Sandra the knife and confessed to murder a little over half an hour later. Sandra retreated in her seat, knocking her chair back into the wall. She stared at Achara, her smiling face, her bloodstained, once white clothing, and then at the knife's glistening blade, spattered with red. The evidence of Sandra's eyes told its own story, a story of destruction, a story of death. But the receptionist found that reality impossible to accept. 'Did I hear you right? Did you say you've killed somebody?'

Achara pointed to the knife. 'Yes, that's right, one of your own, and that's the sacrificial blade right there.'

Sandra's mouth fell open. 'Are you saying you killed a police officer?'

'Yay, she's got it, ten out of ten. I killed a pig. A pig that needed slaying. A pig called Peter. He's lying bled-out in the park. It's far too late to save him. And hooray to that. That's what I say. Hooray to that!'

Sandra hit the panic button hard, pressing herself against the back of her booth, as three uniformed officers rushed into the reception area. Achara held her hands up high. 'Oh, look, it's the three little piggies come to arrest the executioner. I did it. I surrender! I killed your piggy detective friend because God demanded it. Oink, oink, the pig deserved to die.' She lay flat on the reception room's blue-carpeted floor with her arms and legs spread wide, waiting to be arrested, as the officers circled her. Within minutes Achara was cuffed and secured in a cell, awaiting Kesey, as an ambulance transported Best's slowly stiffening body to the morgue.

Achara had shown no remorse, regret or fear. She sat in her cell and sung quietly to herself. All was well with the world. All was exactly as it should be. She began chanting loudly on hearing a key in the lock, metal on metal. 'God is great. I am nothing. All praise to the master. Did you hear me, pigs? God's purpose is served. All praise to the master!'

* * *

Kesey sat alongside Detective Constable Raymond Lewis, with Achara and her overworked duty solicitor on the other side of the small table. The suspect was wearing a white paper boiler suit. Her bloody clothing had been bagged and labelled for forensic evaluation. Kesey glanced sideways at her colleague, looking suddenly older.

She was holding back the tears, but only just. 'Switch the tape on, Ray. It's time we made a start.'

Lewis flicked the switch as instructed.

Kesey stated the time, date and location, and then continued in a wavering voice reverberating with raw emotion. 'My name is

Detective Inspector Laura Kesey. Also present is Detective Constable Raymond Lewis, the suspect Ms Achara Davidson, and Mr Oliver May, her legal representative. I need to remind you, Ms Davidson, that you are still subject to caution. Anything you say could be used in evidence. Do you understand?'

Achara nodded, smiling. She looked relaxed, at ease.

'Say it for the tape, Ms Davidson. We need to hear you say it.'

'Yes, I understand.'

Kesey wanted to shout. She wanted to scream. She wanted to tell her prisoner precisely what she thought of her. To drive home the tragic futility of her actions. To convey the terrible waste of a life. But the detective somehow retained her composure. The rules of evidence were clear. Breaking them could jeopardise the chances of a successful prosecution. And that wasn't an option. Not when the brutal and senseless murder of a friend and workmate was involved.

Kesey took a ten-by-six inch colour photo of the crime scene from a burnt-orange cardboard file. She looked at it briefly and then slid it across the table. 'Can you describe what you can see in the photograph for me, Ms Davidson?'

Achara picked it up, studying the image carefully, tilting her head first to one side and then the other. 'It's a punishment killing. A dead pig. Isn't it obvious? Why do you feel the need to ask?'

'A punishment killing?'

Achara began laughing, the volume gradually getting louder, bordering on the manic. 'Oh, come on, please don't tell me you're that stupid. I killed him. I killed the pig. I sliced his throat. His death was a punishment for interrupting the master's holy work. A bloody sacrifice! It's a beautiful picture. A stunning picture! Everything's exactly as it should be. I'm proud of what I've done.'

The solicitor raised a hand. 'If you could stop there please, inspector. I need to consult with my client.'

Achara turned, craning her neck, placing her face only inches from his. 'Shut up, you ridiculous man. You're here as a witness to my confession, and nothing more. I know exactly what I'm doing. Don't even think about interrupting me again.'

Kesey thanked her lucky stars. 'Just to confirm, Ms Davidson. You admit to killing DC Peter Best. You acknowledge that you murdered him in cold blood in Carmarthen Park earlier this afternoon?'

'I planned the killing, I met the pig, and I killed the pig. I confess. It was my responsibility. Why don't you charge me? God will reward me in heaven.'

Kesey clenched her jaw. 'Who else was involved?'

'It was just God, me and the pig.'

'I don't believe that's true, Achara. This isn't a game. We're talking about murder. You're facing a very long time in prison, twenty, maybe twenty-five years. If someone told you to do it. If someone encouraged you to commit the crime, now's the time to say so. Co-operation is the only card you have left to play.'

'God spoke to me in a dream. I serve the master. But he played no part in the crime. He's innocent of any wrongdoing.'

'I believe the man you refer to as the master influenced you to commit this crime. I'm correct, aren't I? I think you'd do anything he told you to. It's very obvious to me that you're under his spell.'

'God is great. I am nothing. All praise to the master. Nobody was involved but me.'

'Where did you get the knife?'

'I borrowed it from the community kitchen. Perhaps you'd be good enough to return it when you're done with it. I'm sure my brothers and sisters can make good use of it again.'

Kesey clenched and relaxed her fists. 'How did you get from the community compound to Carmarthen before the killing? Did the man you refer to as Baptist transport you? Someone must have known what you were planning.'

'I walked as far as Llandeilo and caught a bus from there. No one else knew, only me.'

'That was a very long way to walk. Are you certain you weren't given a lift? I can check the local CCTV. There's no point in lies.'

Achara looked to the ceiling. 'God gave me strength. And there are no cameras. Perhaps we could bring this farce to a close. I need to pray.'

'If you're protecting someone, you're making the biggest mistake of your life. Have you got any idea what you've done? You've killed a good man, a husband, a father of two young children.'

'All praise to the master. The pig deserved to die.'

Kesey fought to suppress her rage, focussing on achieving a conviction to avoid losing control. 'Tell me how you killed DC Best. Give me the details from start to finish.'

Achara shared the entire story, relishing the telling. 'Do you feel no guilt at all?'

'Why would I? I don't live by society's rules.'

'Thou shalt not kill. What happened to that?'

Achara grinned, her almond eyes dancing from one person to the next. 'Only God's chosen children will survive the coming tempest. Why concern yourself with one pig's death when you're all about to perish?'

'Where's Harry Gilmore, Achara? He's done nothing to harm you. Will you at least tell me that?'

'Oh, you'll see young Shadow soon enough, inspector. But be very careful what you wish for. You may not enjoy your meeting quite as much as you think.'

'Is that some kind of convoluted admission that you know where he is?'

'God is great. I am nothing. All praise to the master.'

Kesey stood, keen to get out of there before her emotions boiled over. 'Switch the tape off, Ray. Let's get her charged and back in a cell.'

Achara looked across at Kesey, giggling. 'Are you giving up, inspector?'

'Get that murdering bitch out of my sight. This interview is at an end.'

23

Harry's physical recovery progressed surprisingly quickly once he was fed, watered and rested in a room adjacent to the one in which he'd met Achara only days before. Within seventy-two hours of leaving his lightless prison, Harry was gaining strength, encouraged by Baptist, who tightly bandaged his injuries, prescribed various exercises on the instruction of the master, and encouraged periods of chanting and intensive prayer.

Harry was finding that activity helped still his troubled mind. Staying busy was a positive. The exercise was invigorating, despite nagging knee pain that wouldn't let up, and he was beginning to accept Baptist's repeated enthusiastic protestations that everything he'd been through had been for his own good. Tough love.

'The master loves you, Shadow. He loves all his children. He would *never* do anything to harm you. Your perceived suffering was a vehicle for growth. Think of your experiences as delivery pains, contractions birthing a new creation. Your dark underground home was a womb of sorts. You went into the ground as a condemned sinner, and came out a shining light, ready to perform God's work. You are chosen. You have a crucial task to perform on behalf of your brothers and sisters. You are blessed, my brother. It is the greatest of honours. Soon our glorious master will give you your orders.'

'I need help, Baptist. I'm still, I'm still getting nightmares. I'm b-back there in the dark, petrified. There were times when I prayed to die.'

'It's all over now. Live in the present and think only of your duty.'

Harry looked up at the big man with pleading eyes. 'I'm experiencing flashbacks, pictures in my head, terrifying images I can't shake off.'

Baptist rested a hand on Harry's shoulder, gentle, supportive. 'Pray to God, my brother. The corruption of your mind is the devil's work. Drive the evil out.'

'Will you ask the master to help me? He could, couldn't he, if he wanted to?'

Baptist gasped, the sound filling the room. 'I hope you're not having doubts again, my brother. Doubts are the work of the devil. They condemn you to hell. I wouldn't want to put you back in the hole. Not after everything you've achieved.'

'No, no, I've got no doubts, none at all. That is *not* what I meant. All praise to the master! I just thought I could get back to my work more quickly if he healed me, that's all. I know he can do it. I've seen it for myself.'

'On your knees, Shadow. On your knees and pray.'

Harry perched on all fours.

'Pray for forgiveness, my brother. Ask for mercy. Dark forces are at work. Pray, or you may succumb.'

Harry supported the bulk of his slight frame on his uninjured knee, linking his hands together and closing his eyes tight shut. 'I confess my sins. Please God, pardon my many weaknesses. Give me strength to accomplish whatever duty the master demands of me.

God is great. I am nothing. All praise to the master!' Harry threw his arms up, opening his eyes wide and looking at the ceiling. He saw his father's face. He saw him floating down, hovering. 'Did you hear me, Dad? Will you intercede on your son's behalf? I need strength, determination. There is work to do. God is great. All praise to the master!'

24

Baptist stood in the dark, hidden by the night. Dense, towering, vertical clouds masking the moon and casting their shadows.

He peered out from behind a low hedge, rubbing his tired eyes and studying a modern, semi-detached house on the opposite side of the leafy street with a burning intensity that made his head ache. The big man checked his white ceramic wristwatch for the umpteenth time, watching the seconds tick by with increasing impatience until precisely 2 a.m.. All was quiet in suburbia. Just as it should be. Just as required. This was it. All the scheming had led to this. His moment of impending glory. It was time to implement the final stages of the master's inspired plan.

Baptist's eager anticipation was raised to a new high as his eyes darted from one window to the next, up, down, from left to right, and back again. But there was little of worth to see. No lights, no clues as to where Kesey slept. Just a door and four windows, as if it were an ordinary building. As if the sacrificial pig wasn't in the house at all.

Baptist checked the street one final time. All was clear. He hung a white cotton bag over one muscular shoulder and rushed across the road, crossing it in three athletic bounds. He was still struggling to decide on the most advantageous potential access point, despite his prayers for guidance. But he opened the metal gate, nonetheless, silently cursing the devil when it squeaked, and then continued down an uneven concrete pathway towards Kesey's front door, one cautious step at a time. Baptist briefly considered knocking. Knocking as hard as necessary to gain her attention, and then dragging her out of the house and towards the van just as soon as she opened the door. But, no, it was too risky, too dangerous. There could be witnesses. Interfering curtain-twitchers in nearby houses. The tribe of the lost, who couldn't begin to comprehend the glorious nature of his quest.

Baptist hurried round the side of the house, passing a child's swing and a red plastic slide, searching for a more suitable entry point away from potentially prying eyes. He tried a side door on the off-chance it would open, but it remained shut however hard he pulled it. He looked under a black rubber mat for a key, but there was nothing to find.

Baptist pictured himself smashing the glass, punching it with a clenched fist or hurling a suitably sized stone, but he ruled both options out almost immediately. What was he thinking? The master had advised caution. He'd demanded success. One pig was dead. Soon it would be time for another. There was no room for error. Not now, not when the stakes were so very high. Every member of the community depended on him, for their survival, and for their salvation too as the end approached. The master had made that perfectly clear. He'd spelt it out with no room for ambiguity. This was his opportunity for greatness. His chance to go down in the annals of community history. Yes, this was it. The moment had arrived. He had to get it right.

Baptist jumped with a start when a dog barked in a far-off street. He dropped down low, watching, listening, for a full two minutes or more until his confidence finally returned. He wanted to hurt that dog. He wanted to stamp down on it, to tear it apart. But he had to forgive. That's what he told himself. He had to drive thoughts of revenge from his mind. There were more pressing matters to address. The pig detective was so very close on the other side of those walls. Now, all he had to do was get her. To serve his purpose.

Baptist made his way to the rear of the building, feeling his heart dance when he discovered that a small conservatory window was partially open. He stared at it, not quite able to believe his luck, but then concluded it was an act of divine providence. Like the crossing of the Red Sea. The Creator was on his side. Intervening to facilitate his success.

He reached up on tiptoes, pulling himself up, reaching in and unfastening the metal clasp, but he couldn't get his arm far enough through the gap to open the more substantial window beneath. Baptist looked around, searching for something to stand on, but there was nothing suitable. He ground his teeth together, increasingly frustrated with every new obstacle, but then he remembered the slide. It was as if a light came on in his head, a revelation. All he had to do was lean the slide against the conservatory wall, use the steps like a ladder, and then utilise the additional height it provided to reach down inside to gain entry. An inspired idea that couldn't fail.

Within a few minutes, Baptist was inside the conservatory and approaching an interior sliding glass door, the cotton bag held tightly in a large and sweaty hand. To his immense relief, the door wasn't locked, enabling him to enter a dimly lit modern kitchen, fitted with cream-coloured units and various up-to-date electrical appliances to either side of the stainless-steel sink. Baptist stood and waited as his eyes slowly adjusted to the semi-darkness. He moved on into the lounge, and then the small blue-tiled hall, where he paused at the base of the staircase, listening for the even slightest sound. For one awful moment, the big man feared the house may be empty. That the pig detective was at work or sleeping somewhere else entirely. He reassured himself that he'd been careful, that he'd followed her to the property, that lights had shone, and that he hadn't seen her leave. But the fear of failure still sent him reeling. She couldn't have sneaked away, could she? No, no, of course she hadn't. She was up there somewhere, blissfully unaware of her pending fate, lost to sleep. He heard the master's voice urging him on. Encouraging him to seize their sacrificial lamb. To show no mercy. To ignore any misgivings planted by the vile demons of hell.

Baptist took a deep breath, removed his white leather sandals, and began climbing the stairs one wary step at a time, flinching at the slightest creak, and repeatedly adjusting the position of his feet in the hope of a silent approach. He reached the landing and stopped, listening as the faint sound of intermittent snoring came from a bedroom to his left at the back of the house. Baptist confirmed the contents of the bag – the cloth, the chloroform – and then crept towards the open door.

Baptist placed one foot in the bedroom, as Kesey rolled over, adjusting her position, sleeping on her back as opposed to her side. He waited for her to settle, removed the top from the bottle, poured approximately twenty-five per cent of the liquid contents onto a white cotton cloth, and approached her sleeping form. He threw the bag and bottle aside as Kesey opened one eye, and then the other.

He went to grab her, but she moved quickly, jumping from the bed, drawing her arm back and striking him a powerful blow to the throat, sending him stumbling backwards and gasping for breath. Kesey kicked out, snap, but he caught her foot, throwing her sideways. She hit a wall, hard. She was dazed, bruised and shaken, but she wasn't ready to give up the fight.

As Baptist loomed over her with the drug-laden cloth in hand, she kicked upwards, bang, striking his groin with the ball of her foot. The big man groaned as he sunk to his knees. But he reached out and grabbed her trailing ankle as she attempted to dodge past him and out of the door. Kesey pulled away, but she stumbled and fell, giving him just enough time to throw himself on top of her, his massive frame pinning her down, face first. Baptist coughed, catching his breath as he raised his upper body, pulling back on her hair, and holding the cloth to her nose and mouth.

Kesey's scream was silenced almost as soon as it began, as he held the fabric still tighter, pressing it firmly to her face until the sweet-smelling compound began to gradually take effect. Kesey continued to struggle, attempting to twist her body, trying to throw him off one way and then the other, but Baptist was too big, too heavy, too strong. Within five minutes, her frantic movements had slowed to a stop. Kesey was alive but unconscious.

Baptist rolled aside, clutching his aching testicles and resting until he eventually felt ready to continue. He dropped the cloth and then looked across at Kesey's sleeping form and smiled. She had no idea what was coming. No comprehension of the personal hell she'd unleashed on herself. Soon she would be a sacrifice. Her blood a life force, offered to God.

He raised himself to his feet, a growing sense of achievement filling him with pride and puffing out his chest. As he picked Kesey up, resting her over one shoulder, he was calling out his praise, no longer fearful of discovery, confident of ultimate success. Baptist collected his discarded items and descended the stairs two steps at a time, performing a tight pirouette at the bottom, spinning Kesey around as she slept, her feet bumping the wall as he turned. He laughed as he slipped on his footwear and opened the front door.

The Student

The clouds had cleared now, blown away by a wind that cooled his skin. It was a good sign, a sign of God's approval. He thought it and believed it as he strolled down the path, out of the gate, onto the pavement and towards the Transit van, a few minutes' rapid walk away in a nearby street, parked under a faulty lamp. Baptist threw Kesey into the back on reaching the vehicle, slamming the rear doors shut and locking them, just in case she woke prematurely and tried to escape.

As he drove back in the direction of Llandeilo, Baptist was chanting, 'God is great. I am nothing. All praise to the master!' His euphoria was virtually orgasmic as he shouted out the words, anticipating his master's happy approval with explosive glee. It was the greatest achievement of his life. His ultimate triumph. Now, all he had to do was get the pig detective back to the compound. And then God would smile on him. Karma in its purest form. Soon there would be a sacrifice. And he'd get his reward.

25

Three adult male members of the community were busy constructing an eight-by-four foot wooden cross on the dry earth to the side of the parade ground, when Baptist drove back through the commune's high-security gates in the early hours of the morning, with Kesey still lying drugged and senseless in the rear of the van. The big man slowed, wound down the window and waved to a group of women and children cheering on the construction process. The group continued cheering as they waved back, becoming increasingly animated by the thought of the sacrificial ceremony to come.

Cameron watched from a lounge window, on tenterhooks, as Baptist slowed almost to a stop and parked on the grass about twenty-five yards away. He rushed out of his private quarters, running towards the van in the glare of the spotlights, as the big man switched off the diesel engine. Baptist was opening the rear doors when his master approached with a wide-eyed look of unbridled anticipation lighting up his features.

'Have you got her?'

Baptist stood aside, repeatedly nodding his confirmation. He had never felt more accomplished or validated. It was the high point of his life. He stood aside and beamed, enabling Cameron to peer into the back of the vehicle.

'There she is master, at your mercy. It all went better than I could have hoped. The pig tried to struggle, but I got her. I did exactly what you told me to do. I am forever your humble servant.'

Cameron looked in at Kesey's sleeping form and performed a little jig of delight. He threw his arms in the air and jumped up and down, first one foot and then the other, raising his knees high, his entire body wobbling with the effort of it all. He continued dancing for thirty seconds more before suddenly stopping, panting hard as he strived to catch his breath. He turned to Baptist after sufficient recovery time had elapsed, and smiled. 'You have done well, my child. God will reward you for your obedience and devotion. Now, let's get the bitch into my quarters. The spare bedroom will serve as an ideal prison cell until the time of the sacrifice.'

Baptist shuffled back a step as various members of the community gathered to look on despite the early hour. 'Am I right in thinking that you don't want me to put her in the hole, master?'

Cameron hissed his words while waving his followers away, ordering them back to their sleeping quarters with small movements of his hand. 'Are you questioning my wisdom?'

Baptist fell to his knees, as the other white-clad members of the community scuttled away to their beds, their earlier feelings of enthusiasm replaced by fear. Baptist looked up at his master with pleading eyes. 'Please forgive my impertinence, master. I simply thought that time spent in the ground may provide her with the opportunity for reflection and prayer before making her final journey.'

Cameron reached out, jabbing a finger towards Baptist's face. 'If

I'd meant the hole, I'd have said the hole. Now get the bitch out of that van and take her exactly where I told you to take her. Do not ever question me again, or it may be your turn to seek absolution. You did well, my brother. But don't sully that achievement by doubting my infallibility. Always remember I speak for God. Doubt is the work of the devil.'

Baptist rose slowly to his feet. 'Please forgive me, master. I am unworthy of your pardon.'

'Get her out of the van, take her to my private quarters, strip her naked, bathe her, apply essential oils, and then tie her up with the ropes I've left on the spare bedroom floor. I want her at her very best when offered as a sacrifice. God expects nothing less.'

'Yes, master, your word is my command.'

'And you'll find a white cotton hood next to the rope. I don't want the bitch seeing a thing. That will be darkness enough. The inability to see will increase her suffering. She deserves that. We can remove the hood as she's led to the cross. Can you imagine? Can you picture the drama of it all? I can't wait to see the look of shock on her smug face when she sees it facing her, and realises her fate.'

Baptist dragged Kesey from the rear of the van by one arm, lifted her and carried her toward the building, as Cameron strolled close behind, calling out his encouragement, 'That's it, my child, that's it, you know what to do with her. Get her ready as instructed. Come on, no dawdling. It's time to get on.'

Baptist took Kesey directly to Cameron's private bathroom, lowering her to the white tiled floor, as his master stood watching from the open doorway.

'Have you decided on a time for the crucifixion, master? I'm looking forward to what's going to be a wonderful day.'

'I must spend time in meditation and prayer. God will tell me when the time is right.'

Kesey began to stir as Baptist started to unbutton her pyjama top. She opened one eye, and then closed it again, bemused by the residual effects of the drug. 'What the... what the... what the hell's happening to me? Janet, is that you, love?' She opened both eyes for a beat, drifting between a confused dreamworld and consciousness. 'Get off me! What the fuck are you doing? Get the, get the fuck off!'

Kesey bucked wildly, but Baptist held on tight. He shoved her away and then punched her hard, using all his immense weight and strength, knocking her senseless with one mighty blow to the chin. It loosened a tooth.

Cameron patted Baptist on his broad back as he rose to his full height. 'Very well done, my child. Your quick reaction was to your credit. I will mention your achievements when I next speak with the Almighty. No doubt He will reward you when He deems it appropriate.'

'Thank you, master, I'm deeply honoured.'

'It is no more than you deserve, my child. Now, I'm tired, continue with your work.'

Baptist tossed Kesey's pyjama top aside, and then moved on to her trousers, tugging them off at the ankles as she lay motionless. Cameron stepped into the bathroom, looking Kesey up and down, studying her naked form. He quickly decided that she was a little old for his tastes. Somewhat long in the tooth. In her early thirties, maybe, or even more. He thought it regrettable, such a terrible shame. She may have provided some sport if a little younger. But look on the bright side. She'd make a more than adequate sacrificial lamb, nailed up on that cross for all to see and appreciate, a silver lining in a dark world of woe. Cameron took one last look at Kesey, concluding she really wasn't to his taste, however vulnerable. It was time to get some rest.

Cameron reached up to tap Baptist on his shoulder, as he

carried Kesey towards the walk-in shower in a corner of the room next to the frosted glass window. 'I'm going to head to my bedroom for a few hours of sleep, my child. Continue with your work and ensure our guest is adequately restrained before you head to bed yourself. I have some thinking to do. I don't want to be disturbed under any circumstances. Have I made myself clear?'

'I'll ensure she's properly secured, master. You can count on me.'

'Oh, and one more thing before I leave you.'

Baptist stifled a yawn, tiredness starting to get the better of him. 'What is it, master?'

'I want you to bring young Shadow here to see me at precisely nine o'clock in the morning. As I said before, I have an important task for him to perform on behalf of our happy group. I'm not entirely persuaded that he's fully accepted his new life here, despite his time spent in the hole. What I have in mind will be the ultimate test of his loyalty. Tomorrow we will find out if we can truly trust Shadow, or not. He's your responsibility, Baptist. For both your sake and his, I'd like to think we can.'

Baptist propped Kesey up in the shower, positioning her at the furthest point from the sliding door. All of a sudden, he wasn't feeling quite so confident. 'Can I ask what Shadow is to do, master? I could wake him now and prepare him in advance. I could ensure he completes whatever is required of him to an acceptable standard.'

Cameron bared his teeth, snarling. 'You will tell him nothing! Do you hear me? The surprise is an essential element of Shadow's challenge. I want to study his face up close when I tell him exactly what's expected of him. That will tell me all I need to know. If he passes the test, he lives, and if not, we're going to need a second cross.'

'That is truly inspired, master, a true reflection of your genius.'
'Thank you, my child.'

Baptist bowed, bending at the waist, lowering his head and staring down at the tiles at his feet. 'God is great. I am nothing. All praise to the master!'

26

Harry entered the master's spare bedroom to be met by the sight of a naked woman, gagged and hooded and tied to the side of the double bed. Baptist slapped Harry hard when he stood to stare. Harry made every effort to hide his feelings of revulsion for fear of another assault.

'Stand to attention, newbie. Stand and wait for the master's arrival. He has important news to share with you. This is an exam you have to pass.'

Harry shifted his weight from one foot to another, unable to settle, as Kesey emitted garbled calls for help, the tight gag rendering her words close to incomprehensible. Harry wanted to help her, as he had River on that terrible day, but he knew the potential consequences of disobedience. And so he stood there, hating himself for his failure to act, following orders, until Cameron entered the room about ten minutes later.

Cameron ignored all present, climbing onto the bed, feigning sleep for almost five minutes before finally opening his eyes and speaking. 'It's a pleasure to see you again, Shadow, my child. It's good of you to come so very promptly. I would introduce you to our new guest, but she's not going to be with us for very long. I don't think it's in your interest to get to know her.'

Harry's earlier doubts were resurfacing to a greater degree with every word Cameron uttered. He looked at Cameron, avoiding his eyes, and then at the woman again, feeling nothing but sympathy. Should he say something? Should he ask? 'What is it you want from me, master?'

Cameron laughed. 'What indeed? What indeed? What do you make of what you see here, Shadow?'

Harry didn't reply.

'Not to worry, my child. I understand the nature of your confusion. Our guest is an agent of evil. A pig who interfered in our business. She is not a woman, despite her shape-shifting appearance. She is a she-devil, inhuman, a demon from hell. Should we let her live or send her to the netherworld? What do you think, my child? What would you do if you had the power to decide?'

Harry wondered why his mouth felt so parched. He searched his mind for something to say. But no words came. He stood there opening and closing his mouth, guppy-like until Cameron eventually spoke again.

'Nothing to say for yourself, my boy. No? Then I'll tell you what I require of you. At precisely eleven o'clock this morning, the she-devil will be taken from this place and nailed to the wooden cross you will have seen outside, as a sacrifice to God. Steel spikes will be driven through her hands and feet, and you, my child, will do the hammering.'

Harry staggered backwards as Kesey fought to free herself, yanking at the ropes to no avail. Harry lost his balance, falling, and sitting on the wooden floor until Baptist dragged him to his feet seconds later.

'I can't, I can't do, I can't do that. Please, I'll do anything, anything but that.'

Cameron fixed Harry with a look that left him cold. 'You will do *exactly* what you're told, or you will suffer the same fate. Think hard, my child. You have time to pray. Are you on the side of good or evil? You can choose life or death. It really is up to you.'

27

Janet dialled and waited, tapping the sole of her shoe against the floor until she heard Sandra say, 'West Wales Police, how can I help you?' what felt like an age later.

Janet gathered her thoughts before speaking. 'Hello, Sandra, it's Janet, Janet Oldfield, Laura's partner.'

'I don't think she's in, sorry. I haven't seen her since yesterday.'

Janet closed her eyes for the briefest of moments. 'Oh, shit, that's the last thing I wanted to hear.'

'What's the problem, Jan?'

'I need to speak to the new chief super.'

Sandra chewed a fingernail. 'He's here, but he's in a meeting. Is it urgent? He's not a man who likes to be disturbed.'

Janet felt her gut spasm. 'Yes, I really do think it is. You'd better put me through.'

'Detective Chief Superintendent Halliday.'

Janet introduced herself, stressing the urgency of her call. 'I'm rather busy at the moment. Can I ring you back?'

Janet began weeping without words.

'Okay, you've got five minutes, and then I really do have to go.'

'I'm worried about Laura.'

'Please try to be more specific. I haven't got all day.'

Janet tightened her grip on the phone. 'I've been staying at my brother's place with our son, because of the dangers posed by the religious maniacs who killed DC Best. I've just arrived home to find Laura's car parked outside the house. But she's not here. And she's not in work either. I've tried contacting her by phone, but I can't get an answer. If she'd left the house of her own free will she'd have left a note. I think there's every chance she needs help.'

Halliday emitted another deep outward breath. 'Do try not to jump to conclusions, Janet. You're very probably worrying about nothing.'

'I really don't think so. I saw a woman dressed in white outside our house. And Laura thought she was being followed. I want you to do something. I need you to take my concerns seriously. If the bastards abducted a student off the street, why wouldn't they take Laura too?'

'Thank you for your information. I'll give it some thought.'

'What the hell's that supposed to mean?'

The irritation in his tone was unmistakable. 'I have a duty of care to DI Kesey, as I do all the officers under my command. The matter will be dealt with appropriately. You can be assured of that. Please do not contact me again unless you have new and relevant information to share.' And with that, he put the phone down.

28

The morning sun bathed the compound in a pale yellow light as Baptist shoved Harry out of the men's dormitory and towards the parade ground, where the many members of the white-clad community were already gathered in a mood of heightened expectation.

Harry was led through the tightly packed crowd to where Kesey was laid out on the large wooden cross, her wrists bound tightly to the crossbar and her ankles to the base. There was a crown of thorns around her head, cutting her skin, and her mouth was gagged with a length of white cloth, limiting her cries of anguish to guttural noises.

Harry looked down at her naked body and began to weep. The master had said she was a she-devil, a demon from hell, but she looked like a woman to him. He continued to stare, caught in indecision until that same trumpet fanfare rang out from the tannoy system, drowning out his thoughts, filling his world with vibrations that travelled through the air and made him flinch. Harry wanted to run as he had on that first day. But like then, there was nowhere to go.

Cameron appeared from his private quarters, dressed in his finery, as the blast of trumpets reached a theatrical crescendo, gradually increasing in volume. The members of the group turned to look at their leader, cheering loudly as they moved aside to allow him to pass. Their master stood at the head of the cross, smiling down at Kesey, appreciating the terror in her eyes for a few seconds more, before finally addressing his followers. 'Welcome, my children. Welcome on this, the greatest of days.'

The resulting cheers, whoops and fevered clapping continued for a full five minutes until Cameron raised a hand and continued. 'Soon, we will sacrifice this worthless creature to the glory of God. And in that act, she will gain redemption. A she-devil will become a sacrificial lamb.'

The cheers were even louder now. Some members of the community danced around, leaping energetically as their excitement reached a state of intense emotion that far exceeded their past experience. They continued yelling, shouting out their praise until Cameron silenced them with a wave of his hand. 'The time is almost here, my children. Very soon, the cross will be raised from the ground. But before then, Shadow has a task to perform on behalf of us all. It is the greatest of honours. An act of loving devotion that will signal his acceptance as a full and exalted member of our merry band.' He met Harry's eyes. 'Shadow, if you would step forward, the time has arrived.'

Harry remained frozen to the spot as Mary slowly approached him to the sound of beating drums, carrying a large, steel claw hammer and four glistening six-inch nails laid out on a white silk-covered cushion.

Harry looked at his master, then at the woman secured to the cross, and then at his master again. He took the hammer in hand, surprised by its weight, gripping the rubber covered shaft with a clammy hand that wouldn't stop trembling. He looked down at the weeping woman one more time, as Cameron shouted his encouragement. 'Drive in the nails, my child. Now is the time. Hammer the nails in! Drive the devil from our midst. This moment will define you for eternity.'

Harry moved quickly, raising the hammer high above his head and bringing it crashing down, splitting Cameron's skull and sending him to the ground, where he twitched and shook, warm blood pouring from a fatal head wound. Every member of the community rushed forwards, led by Baptist, enveloping Harry in a wave of stunned and revengeful violence, as the choppy sound of a distant police helicopter gradually got louder and louder, creating a down-draft that sent people reeling as it appeared overhead.

29

FOUR MONTHS LATER

Kesey handed Raymond Lewis a pint of best bitter and smiled. 'There you go, Ray. That should take the edge off.'

Lewis slurped the malty froth from the top. 'Thanks, boss, I needed that.'

She sipped her lager shandy. 'Right, what the fuck's going on? This is off the record. You can speak freely. You haven't been yourself for weeks. I want to know why.'

Lewis looked up and waved as an old friend approached the Carmarthen Rugby Club bar. 'It's the Cameron case, boss. I still can't get my head around what happened. All that hate. And then the way the bastard died. It was too easy. Where's the justice? He should have been locked up for the rest of his miserable life.'

'We can't win them all, Ray.'

'Yeah, but we should have won that one.'

Kesey looked at him with a thoughtful expression. 'I wouldn't be here now if you hadn't arrived when you did. I'm alive and kicking. I've got you and young Gilmore to thank for that. I'm just grateful the CPS saw sense and didn't bring charges against him.'

He drained his glass to the halfway point. 'How is Harry, any news?'

'Yeah, I was talking to his mother only yesterday, as it happens. He's back in university and having regular counselling. Obviously, he's still shaken by his experiences, he took quite a beating, but Sally said he's feeling more optimistic about the future. I'm still trying to feel the same way.'

'At least that big bastard had a good long sentence.'

'Yeah, he was always going down. There was no way I was letting him slip away. Not after everything he did to me. He'll be in his seventies by the time he's released. And that's if he lives that long. Twenty-three years is a long stretch for someone in their fifties.'

'You did well, boss.'

'It was touch-and-go for a while.'

Lewis gulped his beer. 'What did you make of the Thai girl's insanity defence?'

'Achara? She grew up in an abusive household. And then she was sucked in by Cameron's crowd. But I'm still not persuaded. I think she knew exactly what she was doing.'

'They can always transfer the bitch to prison if they decide it's a con job.'

Kesey nodded. 'Yeah, I guess so.'

He looked at her with a sideways glance. 'They're not all con men, you know, not all of them.'

'What?'

'Healers, there are genuine ones out there. They're not all psychos like Cameron.'

Kesey smiled tentatively. 'Where the hell did that come from?'

'My sister was diagnosed with breast cancer a few years back. It had spread. There was nothing the doctors could do. Three months they said, and that was at best. And then a friend of a friend recommended a healer in London. I was sceptical, she was sceptical, but it worked. She's still with us, and the cancer hasn't come back. I wouldn't have believed it if I hadn't seen it for myself.'

'You never fail to surprise me, Ray. That was the last thing I was expecting you to say.'

He looked away. 'How's Janet? I haven't seen her since the Christmas piss-up.'

'Are you changing the subject?'

He grinned. 'Yeah, I suppose I am.'

'She's still trying to talk me into changing jobs every chance she gets. You know, for something less stressful, something safer.'

'It's not surprising if you think about it. She nearly lost you.'

'Yes, I know. And not for the first time.'

'You're not actually considering it, are you?'

Kesey shook her head. 'No, not a chance, I'm a copper through and through. Always have been, and always will be. No one's going to change that. Not Cameron, not Baptist, and not any of the other scumbags out there.'

'That's good to hear.'

'While we're here, Ray, I'm planning to recommend you for promotion, if you're up for it?'

Lewis grinned. 'About bloody time. I thought you'd never ask.'

'We've got a new case. It's going to be high profile. It's something I want us to work on together.'

Lewis emptied his glass in one generous swallow. 'Get the beer in and tell me all about it. I've got all the time in the world.'

MORE FROM JOHN NICHOLL

We hope you enjoyed reading *The Student*. If you did, please leave a review.

If you'd like to gift a copy, this book is also available as an eBook.

Sign up to John Nicholl's mailing list for news, competitions and updates on future books.

https://bit.ly/JohnNichollNews

The Cellar, another shocking and addictive psychological thriller by John Nicholl, is available to order now.

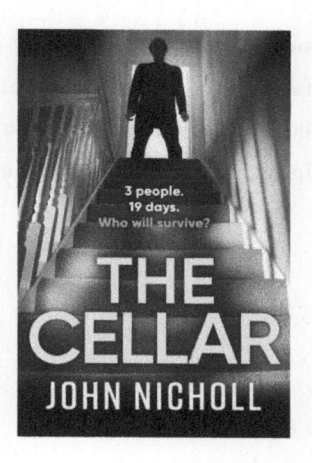

ABOUT THE AUTHOR

John Nicholl is an award-winning, bestselling author of numerous darkly psychological suspense thrillers, previously published by Bloodhound. These books have a gritty realism born of his real-life experience as an ex-police officer and child protection social worker.

Visit John's website: https://www.johnnicholl.com

Follow John on social media:

- twitter.com/nicholl06
- facebook.com/JohnNichollAuthor
- bookbub.com/authors/john-nicholl
- instagram.com/johnnichollauthor

Boldwood

Boldwood Books is an award-winning fiction publishing company seeking out the best stories from around the world.

Find out more at www.boldwoodbooks.com

Join our reader community for brilliant books, competitions and offers!

Follow us
@BoldwoodBooks
@BookandTonic

Sign up to our weekly deals newsletter

https://bit.ly/BoldwoodBNewsletter

Milton Keynes UK
Ingram Content Group UK Ltd.
UKHW041336240724
1018UKWH00077B/1564

9 781804 263891